# THE FIRE IN THE ICE

D.M. MARLOWE

Cover Design by Chris Cocozza

❀ Created with Vellum

*To Tammy and Thomas, Mei's best cheerleaders!*

# CHAPTER 1

There it was again. Just a flicker in the corner of his eye.
Reik sighed. He was a hunter. A scout. A warrior.
*Not* prey, not even for the most powerful of the *yokai*, the spirits and supernatural creatures he was trained to fight. His temper spiked and he stomped on through the snow, willing to give whatever-it-was the chance to smarten up and leave him alone.

Clearly it was not so smart, though, for it continued to follow as the afternoon wore on.

For long stretches, though, Reik would almost forget his stalker. This part of British Columbia was beautiful. A rugged rock, conifer and snow-covered winter wonderland that made him feel right at home. It was also remote—and perfect for crossing the border and getting back to the States, without attracting any kind of attention.

He paused, knowing he was growing close, as the sun began to sink behind the mountains. But it started to snow as he topped a ridge and gazed into a pretty valley below—and his shadow was still with him.

He would stop for the night, deal with the flicker nipping at his heels, and get some rest.

Not a bear or a wolf—or anything mortal. He could feel it hanging at the edge of the wood while he worked to cut some feathery hemlock boughs for a lean-to. Standing back, he evaluated the finished shelter, placing an extra branch here and there to fill in the holes. He didn't feel the cold, but he liked to have the wind off his face while he slept—and he didn't care for the conspicuous—and isolating—nature of a modern tent. The hemlock would catch the snow and form an insulating wall without cutting off his ability to sense what lived in the night around him. He would sleep better that way—after he rid himself of his shadow.

The sun slipped all the way behind the peaks and night rushed into the valley. The sleepy birdsong died away and small rustles and movements in the brush intensified. He built a fire before his shelter—because that's what an ordinary mortal would do. Hunkering down before it, he waited.

It took its time. He never heard a whisper of snow falling from a disturbed branch or saw a footprint appear in the white expanse, but he could feel it drawing closer. He was born of a spirit himself and that part of him surged at the familiar brush of its own kind.

Closer. No sign of it announcing or showing itself.

How impolite.

His senses stretched, his nerves had gone as taut as a pulled bowstring—and then he felt it—the brush of air behind him, a sense of something looming . . .

He didn't turn. Didn't dive out of the way. He merely pointed a finger over his shoulder and shot whatever-it-was with a blast of arctic winter.

A gasp. A grunt. The sound of a struggle. Slowly, Reik rose and spun around to face his stalker.

Huh. This was a new one on him. It snarled at him from a

flat, vaguely humanoid face in a round plate of bone surrounded by a great ruff of hair. A sweeping set of antlers rose above and the powerful, big-boned skeletal outline of a caribou-like creature stretched out behind. More fur ringed the base of the neck and the end of the tail, but none of the bones were attached to each other, they floated in the darkness, moving in concert as if by magic.

Magic, indeed. His icy blast had caught the animal in the region where its chest would be, immobilizing its front end and freezing its forefeet to the ground.

Reik waited. Many spirits, if captured in their physical forms, were unable to phase back until they were freed. But not all.

Judging from the cursing and the frantic struggling as it tried to pull free, this one was caught.

"Talk," he ordered. "What's your deal? Why have you been following me all day?"

It answered only by straining and trying to stab him with a sweep of its antlers.

In return, he stepped back, aimed a hand at it and encapsulated it in a massive block of ice.

It blinked at him once, through the transparent layers, and then it was Reik's turn to flinch, as the creature abruptly transformed, shrinking down and morphing before his eyes into a large, snarling arctic wolf.

The wolf was smaller than the massive caribou form, which left a hollow space inside the ice block. The creature scrambled and leapt as best as it could, trying to break out.

Reik placed a hand on the ice and filled in the hollow spaces inside.

The creature changed again, shrinking again into an arctic hare with a black nose and black tips to its ears. It didn't wait for Reik to react, but shifted immediately again, exploding outward into the form of a polar bear, its eleven-foot-long, powerful body shattering the ice as it roared in triumph.

Reik waited while it rose, roaring, on its back feet to loom threateningly—before he froze it again.

He could feel the fury rolling off it in waves. It tried again, shifting to a fox, then a moose. Reik encased the moose, right up to the massive spread of antlers. "Want to keep going?" he asked snidely. "I can do this all night."

The moose huffed, fogging the ice around its snout. Reik waved a hand and the ice disappeared from the creature's mouth to just above its eyes.

"Let's have a discussion," he suggested. "You have not been very friendly, you know. And here's me, a stranger in these parts." He shook his head chidingly.

"I would have been less friendly still, had I known what you are," the creature spat.

"What I am?" he repeated.

"*Ice mage.*" Clearly this was the worst accusation the creature could imagine. It looked as if the words tasted foul on their way out.

"That's *not* what I am, exactly, but it's no matter. What does matter is that you tell me what your problem is."

The moose snorted.

Reik sighed. "Listen, just come out with it, okay? Either you can tell me or I can leave you here and freeze this entire valley. I don't care what form you take, you won't get out until the spring thaw."

Abruptly, the creature transformed once more and sank back into the space left open within the ice block. Reik stared. It looked mostly human. Inuit, perhaps, as it was dressed in caribou hide and fur. But its eyes—they were wrong. Situated on the vertical, rather than the horizontal, so when it blinked up at him, it blinked sideways.

"What *are* you?" he breathed.

"Ijirac," it muttered, its tone muffled behind the ice. "What are you, if not an ice mage?"

He waved the question away. He had a vague recollection of the story of the Ijirac, although he was more familiar with the Japanese *yokai* than any other creatures of legend and folklore. The Inuit spoke of these creatures, territorial shape shifters who messed with the heads of any hunter too close to their lands. And if he recalled correctly, they were sometimes accused of kidnapping children. "I thought you lived in the far north?"

"We were created in the far north. We live where we like."

And yet all of its transformations had been animals and creatures from the northern reaches.

It looked steadily at him from within the ice. "What side are you on?" it asked abruptly.

The question startled him. And made him feel uncomfortably warm. "Side of what?" he asked casually.

The shook his head. "You know." It waved a hand. "We all know. The war is coming. The dark forces gather and the Mother has chosen her champion. You must choose a side. We all must choose."

A shiver ran up Reik's spine, to hear this creature talk about something that for years only the small group of ninja he'd grown up with had believed. "I'm on my own side, generally."

The strange sideways eyes narrowed. "Those days are gone. But I should have known that an ice mage would stay selfish to the last. You have ice in your veins, I am sure, just like your master."

"My master?" Reik's head came up.

"Yes. I know you were amongst the Tornit, asking questions about White Shoulders." It paused and spoke pointedly. "And I know that White Shoulders is just a masquerade."

Reik kept his expression neutral, but his brain was turning. He *had* been farther north, among the Tornit—the Inuit word for Yeti, Sasquatch or Big Foot. He was indeed trying to find that certain Tornit creature reputed to sport white hair that flowed down over its shoulders to blend with the darker fur below—but he'd thought he'd been the only one to know that White Shoulders might be more than just a Yeti.

His hand rose almost of its own volition and he aimed it at the creature. "What do you know of White Shoulders? Are you allies?"

The Ijirac recoiled. "No." It pushed up against the prison of ice. "You have mastery over the same forces. You must be allied with him, yes?"

"No," Reik answered flatly. "I am no friend to White Shoulders." He stared hard at the creature. "What else do you know of him? Do you know where to find him?"

The Ijirac hunched its shoulders and looked away.

It knew. "Tell me."

"Why would I?"

"Because if you know where he is, you were not following me to find him. You had some other reason. And you thought I was allied with him. What did you mean to do? Kill me? Capture me and hold me hostage? Either way, you meant to harm *him* through *me*." He drew in a deep breath. "Tell me where he is and I'll do it for you."

"Why? What is he to you?"

"An enemy," Reik bit out. The didn't need to know any more.

"And what do you mean to do, should you find him?"

He'd spent years imagining it. "He has something that doesn't belong to him. I am going to take it back."

The creature made a noise of disgust.

Reik laughed softly. "Believe me, he won't like losing it. But I'll punish him, too. If I can find an elegant and devastating way to do it."

The Ijirac studied him for a moment, then shook its head. "You still hide something. I cannot trust you."

"Oh, I'm hiding many things—and so are you. Why do you wish him harm?"

"I mean only to pay him back for the pain he has cost another," the creature spat.

"Funny. That's exactly my mission."

"You share his powers. Surely he will have taught you. *Humans*," it said in disgust. "Am I to expect you to keep your word to me when clearly you have broken whatever pact you made with him?"

"Pact? Taught me?" Reik curled his lip. "I've never laid eyes on him, not in any form. And he will regret the day that I do."

"Never met him?" The Ijirac considered this. It frowned and narrowed its strange eyes. "I did see your hair when you stopped this afternoon and removed your parka."

Reik scowled.

The sideways gaze narrowed again. "I see."

Did he? Reik hoped not. He'd kept his white hair covered when he'd been among the Tornit, and though their gazes had lingered on the markings on his face, they hadn't pried. Nobody knew his secret. He hated the idea of it out there. Beyond him and his mother. *Known.*

"A blood feud." The creature nodded his head. It paused, waiting for Reik to deny the statement.

Reik said nothing.

"It is a powerful thing." Abruptly, it stood. "Yes. I will tell you. And you will let me go."

"I will let you go if you vow never to mention me—to anyone." Reik stepped close to the ice and met the creature's gaze directly. "And if you will not vow, then I will bury you in the bottom of a glacier."

"No, no!" The Ijirac raised his hands. "I will vow! And I

will send you to do your worst to the ice mage." It nodded again. "A fitting vengeance it is for me, to send his son to strike him down." He flourished his arms. "Let me out and I will tell you just how to find him."

With a flourish of his own, Reik blew the ice out and away from the creature. "I'm listening."

# CHAPTER 2

N*o. No. No.*
    *So. Not. Right.*

Reik perched in a silver fir and stared in dismay.

The location wasn't the problem. The Ijirac had given detailed directions. Reik had been surprised to hear that Runar, the ice mage—also occasionally known as White Shoulders, the Yeti—spent his winters on the high slopes of Mount Rainier, near Seattle. He'd found the spot easily enough, though.

It looked similar to a thousand other locations above the snow line of the active volcano. A rocky ridge curved to create a sheltered spot, framed on the other side by a small, frozen expanse of ice. Literally a glacier, if not on the scale of the larger Nisqually, Emmons and other ice expanses up here on the high slopes. Together, the ridge and the ice framed an oblong circle of open space. A stand of mixed evergreens stood to the left of the ice flow and another grew to the right and slightly behind the ridge. Tucked up inside the curve of the rocks he could see the mouth of a cave.

Snug enough—and not what had sent disappointment and dismay oozing like sludge through his gut.

No—that would be the fault of the figure moving about the snowy space before the cave.

Reik was sure that every kid who grew up without a father dreamed of what his missing parent would look like, once found. And guaranteed—no kid imagined his dad as ordinary. *Everyone else's father might be balding with a potbelly, by my dad will be different.*

Reik had more reason to think so than most. He knew damned little about him, but he did know his father was old —an ancient being with command of water and ice. Reik had pictured him often—sometimes as an aging rock-star type, whippet-thin and strong, with tattoos and big hair like an old-time musician.

Other times he'd imagined a robed, larger-than-life glowing figure, like a boss from a vid-game, with burning eyes and an icy staff.

He'd never imagined this—this boring, stocky, regular-looking guy, carefully building a fire, chanting and fussing over it like an old woman. You'd never fight this guy in a game-ending duel—he would only be cast as a background extra in a vid game—one that dealt with Vikings or some other barbarian horde.

Granted, his hair was . . . interesting. The sides of his head were shaved. The thick, white hair on top was long and braided and swept back into a segmented ponytail that reached down his back and was wrapped in multi-colored leather strips.

But that was the only bit of bad-assery about him. He was short. Shorter even than Reik. Neither clean-shaven nor bearded, but a strange, in-between state of bristly grey. He wore a coat of leather so ragged that the runes and symbols stitched into it looked to be the only things holding it together. Heavy hide boots, sealskin pants and a mangy looking fur thrown over his shoulders finished out his homeless woodsman look.

Not what Reik had pictured when his mother finally confessed that his father was a powerful ice mage.

Swallowing his disappointment, Reik settled in to wait and watch. It should feel familiar. As a scout of Ryu, the hidden ninja village, he'd been sent on hundreds of missions. He'd tucked in to watch and learn about lots of different *yokai* bent on messing with humans. He'd sometimes been set to watch other spirit creatures, followers of the powerful dark spirit, Inaba, who had for hundreds of years plotted farther reaching and more significant harm.

Those were nearly always spiritual beings, though, and Reik had to admit, he'd grown used to having the advantage of a spirit legacy in his work. His heritage gave him an affinity to his prey and an edge that he'd never confessed to. It didn't help him now, though. Runar was not quite human, but neither was he a spirit. He was some sort of hybrid, imbued with magic from a different source. Reik had to operate blind on this mission, just like every other scout had to do every day.

Thoughts of Ryu always soured his mood. Sheer boredom tanked it. Runar only seemed interested in the careful tending of his fire and the pot he'd placed over it. It took a couple of hours before Reik suddenly straightened. He was slipping. It had taken him this long to realize that the old man had shuffled around the clearing all day, yet the snow remained smooth and pristine. Narrowing his eyes, Reik could see not even one footprint.

He knew how to smooth out his own footprints, after the fact, but he'd never seen the mage pause to cast such a spell. Carefully checking the angle of the sun, Reik pulled out a small set of binoculars. He waited for the man to move away from the pot and focused his lenses on his feet.

Runar and his heavy boots *were* leaving footprints in the snow, but they filled in of their own accord as soon he stepped away—and had disappeared entirely before he'd gone farther than a step or two.

Reik was impressed, despite himself. It might seem small, but this was powerful, constantly depleting magic. Reik could probably do it, with intense concentration. Runar appeared to accomplish it without conscious effort.

He sharpened his gaze then, and began to notice other things. The cold, biting breeze that stirred the branches of Reik's tree did not appear to be blowing near the cave at all. Small trees and a hanging linen towel never stirred. Even the un-matted bits of the man's fur wrap lay quiet and undisturbed.

The ridge wasn't high enough to deter all wind. A weather block? A force field? Either would be a serious drain on Reik to sustain. Yet Runar looked relaxed and utterly focused on the contents of his pot.

Either he was extremely powerful, or he was a seriously accomplished multi-tasker.

The light began to fade. Runar crumbled a last few bits of something into his pot and flames flared high. The ice mage stood straight and tossed off his fur wrap. Dipping out a bowl full of his concoction, he lifted it high and started another low, sonorous chant.

With deliberate steps that kept time with his chanting, the ice mage crossed to the western side of the clearing. He bowed to the setting sun, straightened, and flicked his fingers into the bowl, spreading drops of his potion around him. He then marched to each compass point in the clearing, contin-uing his chant and his offering drops of steaming liquid.

The chant stopped as the sun touched the first peak on

the horizon. Runar spun and went back to the fire, walking in a circle around it and pouring the rest of the contents of the bowl as he went.

He started his song again as he stopped and cast the bowl aside. Bending, he gripped the large pot and held it aloft.

Reik winced. He assumed the man was protecting his hands, otherwise he would be badly burned. But the ice mage merely bent at the knees, straightened with an unintelligible shout, and sent the contents of the pot soaring aloft.

He must have hit it with a blast of dry arctic air at the same time. The potion instantly evaporated into a spectacularly jagged fan of reddish-tinged cloud.

Perhaps that was what the weather block was for?

Runar stood, arms spread and still singing, until the cloud drifted aloft and disappeared into the darkening sky. Once it was gone, he bent, gathered up his pot and bowl, and entered the cave.

Reik stayed where he was. He watched the fire die down and wondered what Runar was up to. Something had happened when that potion had condensed into vapor. He'd felt the surge of power. But what did it mean?

Full dark fell and Runar had not emerged from the cave. Reik stretched. It was time for him to seek shelter too. Climbing down, he jumped the last few feet—and froze as he felt another, small spike of magic.

The tree above him shuddered. Literally. It shook, all of its branches moving, and all of the snow that had gathered on them abruptly fell with a muffled *whomp*.

He fixed his eyes on the mouth of the cave, but nothing moved. No sign of Runar. With a silent curse, Reik fled.

It appeared his father was not as oblivious as he'd thought.

# CHAPTER 3

Reik was awake and back before dawn, but still Runar was up and investigating before him.

Skidding to a stop a good distance away, Reik ducked behind a tree. He waved a hand to erase his trail and watched the ice mage circle the tree where Reik had perched the day before. The man walked all the way around, studying the ground, the green branches bared of their snow, and eyeing the view of his cave from the spot. Over his shoulder he carried a large sack, partly filled with something that weighted the bottom.

As Reik stared, the mage set the bag aside. He stood motionless for a moment, then suddenly flung his arms out. Light shone under his skin. It *moved*, in a sickening whirl, and then flashed bright. When it faded, Runar was gone—and White Shoulders stood in his place.

Reik ducked behind the tree. Quick as a wink he pulled moisture from the air and covered himself head to foot in a thin film of ice. The Yeti was huge. It wasn't all hair, either. He'd seen the creatures wrangle trees as big as that one out of the ground. They had the muscle to match their size. And despite the incredibly rank aroma coming off him, Reik knew the creature possessed a powerful sense of smell.

And yes, even from here and through the icy film, he could hear the deep breathing and quick sniffing sounds the Yeti made as it inspected the tree again. Holding utterly still, he hoped it wouldn't scent him here.

Several long moments passed. Reik didn't move a hair. He barely breathed. It wasn't until several moments later that he heard the sound of footfalls—moving away from his position.

Waiting, waiting, he held still. At last he peeked around the tree, just in time to see the Yeti moving quickly up the ridge, his bag once more slung over his shoulder.

Still, Reik waited. Not until a while later, when a squirrel scrambled overhead and the birds started twittering among themselves again, did he break the film of ice and move out from his hiding spot.

His senses on alert, he crept toward the clearing and the cave. Runar knew he was here. He knew *someone* was here, in any case. There might be another warning spell set up. Or a booby trap.

The thought came just as he reached the curved and trailing edge of the mountain ridge. He stopped and listened. He tested the wind. Nothing. Cautiously, he put his foot down past the last few rocks that had fallen from the stone ridge. It may not have been marked, but it was the implied edge of Runar's clearing.

A soft sounding *whump* was his only warning, then Reik was ducking, throwing up a shielding blast of sleet-filled air.

The shield held as he was bombarded from two sides. Large, hard-packed snowballs hit, one after the other. Two, four, from both sides they came, until at least a dozen of them had struck his shield, broke apart, then slid down to pile up around him.

He stared. Had he been anyone else, he'd now be buried in a heavy mound of snow. He looked wildly about to see where they had come from—and saw the trees to the side of the ridge swaying madly, as did the ones in the small copse lining the other side of the ice across the clearing.

Runar had spelled *trees* to pelt him with an avalanche of snowballs? Reik shook his head. This was magic beyond his experience.

Suddenly he froze. Footsteps. Heavy, fast and heading this way.

Already unnerved, Reik panicked. He ran back the way he'd come, waving his hand to erase his footprints as he went. He was beyond the Yeti's clearing, making his way though the forest when he heard a roar of fury and frustration behind him. Heart pounding, he raced back to the small, dry hollow he'd found and covered with the fall of an aromatic cedar.

He stayed there the rest of the day, and all the next day, too. It wasn't until the second afternoon had begun that he caught a whiff of a horrid scent. Immediately, he sealed off the mouth of his retreat with a wall of ice.

He was well hidden. He'd gone to some trouble to make it look as if the cedar had toppled due to natural causes. If White Shoulders couldn't scent him past the smell of the cedar and his barrier, it should have no cause to look further.

He only hoped it would leave before he ran out of air.

Tucked in and blind, he wondered how he would know.

Suddenly he pressed himself against the stony wall of the hollow. The cedar tree was moving. Bouncing and swaying— as if something heavy was pulling it—or walking upon it.

But then his eyes widened and he braced himself hard. More than just the tree was moving. The floor rumbled, vibrating madly—and so did the wall behind him.

The mountain! It was so easy to forget, above the snow

line, with the glaciated peak above, that it was an active volcano beneath their feet.

The cedar's branches stilled. Another jolt beneath his feet —as if something heavy landed nearby—and then a long, warbling call sounded outside, loud enough for him to hear through his barrier.

Silence.

He waited until the air in the cave had gone noticeably bad before he released the wall of ice at the front.

Nothing. Moving slowly, listening intently, he ventured forward to peek through the branches.

White Shoulders had gone.

For about sixty seconds, Reik allowed himself to just wallow in relief—and then he started packing up. Confronting his father—it was going to be difficult enough. He didn't want to do it until he had what he came for—and he would vastly prefer to face him in his human form. Runar —the man—was going to be the greatest challenge he'd ever faced. With the Yeti there was a chance he'd never reach the challenge. The creature might just squash him first and ask questions later.

It took only minutes for him to gather his things before he set off. He'd waited his whole life for this, the one mission that really meant something to him. So it wasn't going as easily as he'd hoped? No problem. He could be just as wily and tenacious as his father.

It started to snow as he began to move down the mountain. He carefully removed most of his prints as he went, but he also left a strategic imprint of a boot edge—here. And stuffed a bit of aromatic jerky wrapper in a tree snag—there.

Let his father believe he had chased him off the mountain. Reik was still plotting—and he was being very careful.

He was also going to call in reinforcements.

# CHAPTER 4

The snow grew heavier, slowing Reik's retreat, but he kept going until he reached the level of one of the human habitats on Rainier's slopes. The Paradise was a rustic inn, situated at an elevation of fifty four hundred feet. Between the storm and the time of year, it stood quiet and deserted. Still, Reik kept moving, avoiding the roads and moving deeper into the forest.

The light was fading fast when he reached a snow-covered clearing. He paused. There would be no handy caves or depressions here. But it was secluded and quiet—and he thought it was far enough away from Runar's territory. So he put forth a little effort, using his talents to make solid bricks of snow and piled them in a spiral shape, leaning in slightly, forming them into a snug igloo as his Inuit friends had taught him. He brought in a pile of twigs to lay his blankets over. Checking to be sure that the smoke escaped as it should, he started a fire and a pot of camp ration stew.

When at last he was full and settled, he settled down into a meditative position, pulled out a mirror, centered himself, and put out the call.

Scrying took skill. Losing yourself, drifting into the . . . ether, for lack of a better word for the space *in between.* Finding a tendril of the person or creature you sought, following it until it turned to a thread. Harder still was it to let loose a part of yourself, to open up and send your need along the line to act as a summons.

Reik was good at it, though. He was quick to find his targets and strong enough to get his message across clearly. His calls were always answered quickly.

But not this time.

He lingered. He could feel the line—but he couldn't sense where it led. Couldn't make contact. Why? He gave the thread a good mental tug, but stare as he would into his mirror, there was no answer.

Frustrated, he blinked himself awake and fully back into his body. The fire had burned down to embers. It had grown late. Yawning, he scrubbed his eyes and determined to try again in the morning.

He built up the fire for company, then curled up on his bed of twigs and blankets. Watching the flames, he drifted toward sleep. He heaved a deep, tired sigh, and it seemed but a moment later that he plunged into a dream.

He'd had this one before. Many times, but not for a while, now. In the dream, he was young. Four or five years old, perhaps. He lived in JanFran still, in Inaba's complex, built in the rubble left of the once great city of San Francisco.

It started like every other dream—like every other day he'd spent in the laboratories. His handlers talked to him through glass walls. *Make it snow*, they would command. *Call up a fog. Make it storm. Fill the room with wind and stinging ice.*

As his experience and talents grew, the white-coated men would come into the room, carrying objects with them. Weapons, for the most part. *Cover it in ice. Make one from ice.*

*Make the ice stronger, harder. Make it unbreakable. Make it so that it will never melt.*

He'd been confused many times during those sessions. Did they not understand? Ice was ice. It shattered and melted as it was meant to. Why did they want him to ask it for more?

Those days tired him out. When they had finished with him, they would take him back and leave him in his colorless, windowless room. He would lie in bed, droopy-eyed and waiting. Hoping.

On the good nights, she would come. His mother. Yuki Onna. The Snow Woman. The ancient *yokai* that Inaba had changed, trapped into a half life of bondage.

She was beautiful. Remote. But she was gentle with him. Her touch was cool and soothing. She would take him into her lap and brush his hair and he would close his eyes in bliss. On the nights that he cried, she would catch the pellets of his frozen tears and sprinkle them over his head until he laughed.

No one knew she came. He was not to speak of it. And he never would, because he lived for those nights.

It was she who first taught him to use his talents. He'd been so very small when she started to play their games—she showed him how to summon a snowball out of the thin air. They would toss it back and forth, and he would add layers until it grew too big to handle. His skills grew with him and she made it fun. No orders over an intercom, or scribblings on clipboards, no attached wires and endless starts and stops. With her it was just play. Chasing winds and being tossed into snow banks. Small smiles and eyes lit with pride and pleasure.

He loved her. He loved those nights. But he didn't always love to revisit them.

But tonight's dream—something was different.

The dream started the same. His mother came in. She stroked his hair and let him climb into her lap. But then she set him down, took him by the hand and led him out of his room.

He'd never dreamed this before. Certainly, it had never happened in real life. She held on to him as they walked, leaving the sterile lab environment and heading into the residential part of Inaba's palace.

Guards stood at intervals, but seemed not to see them. The hallways grew wider, the carpets thicker. His mother led him to a lavish bedchamber, filled with art, armor and rich fabrics. It was empty of life, however.

Inaba's? It must be, for there was the elaborately framed, large mirror. The specially spelled mirrors were Inaba's windows into the real world.

In the dream, Reik looked around with wonder and disbelief that belonged to him now, not to his younger self. So much luxury for a creature that could not cross out of the spirit plane, despite centuries of obsessive attempts.

But perhaps the room served other purposes. His mother crossed to a dimly lit corner. The flocked wallpaper depicted an elaborate scene from Imperial Japan. She pressed a finger to a depiction of a loyal retainer bowing to his daimyo—and a large section of the wall slid down and a lighted box extended out into the room.

Incongruous—that's what the contents were. Not jewels or money or papers, instead it looked like so much junk. But then she reached down and chose an object—and he knew.

A snow globe. *The* snow globe—the one caged about with decorative scrollwork, the one that held a tiny representation of her inside, her hair floating amongst the snowflakes.

The reason he'd come to the mountain.

She held it up, close to his face in the dream.

*I know*, he wanted to say. Impatient. *I know what it is. The object that tethers you.* But he couldn't seem to talk in this dream.

She held it up again and the fluid inside swirled in a multi-colored maelstrom. He frowned—and suddenly he was there, lost, awhirl inside the storm.

His mother was beside him. She waved a hand—and the colors parted. Below them lay a vivid landscape. He blinked. It looked remarkably like a live version of the wallpaper's images. Green fields, carts on rutted roads, a tiny village of small houses and a larger, tile-roofed temple in the distance.

Reik frowned again—

And awoke.

He bolted into a sitting position, but the dream was already fading. The feeling of urgency stayed with him, though, and he scrubbed the sleep out of his eyes, took up his mirror and tried scrying again.

With no better results than he'd had last night. With a groan of frustration, he tossed the mirror aside. "Why doesn't he answer?"

"Because I don't do scrying anymore, dude."

Reik jumped up, craning his neck. The voice had come from above.

"It's not safe. I told you so, the last time I saw you. Don't you listen?"

Reik frowned up at the smoke hole, where a baleful eye glared down at him. "And I'll tell you now, as I did then, that you are just being paranoid." He crawled out of the igloo and put his hands on his hips, staring at the creature atop the structure. "We've all been scrying for hundreds of years. Privately and safely. No one has ever been able to hijack it before, Daisuke. Why should it be different now?"

"Times, they are a-changing, Reik."

His friend jumped down and stood before him, grinning. His friend who just happened to be a Nue.

The creature's monkey face grinned at Reik, from just below the level of his own head. The shoulders attached to the tiger's legs gave a shrug. "Strange and disturbing is the new old and boring." The snake that formed his friend's tail hissed at him.

"But paranoid is still paranoid," Reik deadpanned.

Daisuke laughed, but shook his head. "Dude, how long have you been wandering alone out here?"

Reik shrugged. "A while."

"A good while, I'd say. Too long—or maybe not long enough. The wagons are circling back in the real world. The lines are being drawn. Weird stuff is going down, popping up, and jumping in sideways. Nothing is the same anymore—and nothing is safe."

Reik's eyes closed. "Is it so close, then?"

"War is damned close and coming quicker every day." He glanced around in speculation. "This spot's not remote enough to stay hidden, if that's what you are thinking. But if you want to find a better one . . . I'd consider joining you."

Reik winced. "I wish I was only hiding—but I'm about to kick up a hornet's nest of trouble."

"And you need my help?" His friend's snake tail lashed, fangs bared. "Who are we fighting?"

"No." Reik shook his head. "You know I would never force you to pick a side—not even mine. I hate to ask for anything at all—"

"I'm on your side, Reik, just as I know you are on mine. You know you only have to ask."

Reik raised a brow. "I know—but I admit, I did wonder, when I heard a Nue had joined in the attack on Ryu."

"Not me—and you already knew it or you would never have called me." A mocking look crossed his expressive monkey face. "So I know you don't hold that against me—just as I didn't get my back up when that old Nue was defeated at Ryu—and then banished to the back of the spirit world."

"Someone at Ryu defeated him so soundly?" Reik asked, surprised.

"No—someone *from* Ryu. Someone who happens to be living in Inaba's court."

He absorbed that news silently. He knew what his friend was saying and whom he was referring to. He'd wondered what would happen when his mother fetched Akemi back to Inaba instead of Mei—the dark spirit's real enemy. And the Snow Woman had made the switch at his request. He supposed that meant that whatever mischief Akemi got up to under Inaba's influence could be laid at his door.

"That little girl used an old weapon—one designed to take down a Nue," Daisuke continued pointedly. "It's a technique known by damned few these days."

"Well, maybe I did mention it at Ryu, sometime," he said, with a sheepish shrug. "I'm glad you aren't holding it against me—but I won't blame you if do."

The Nue raised one great, wide tiger's paw and Reik immediately placed his hand against it. "We've pulled each other out of too many scrapes to stop now." Daisuke chuckled. "Anyway—I'm glad enough not to have to battle that old crank pot of a Nue on this side of the spirit world."

"Why should you?" Reik asked.

His friend stared. "If I have to pick a side—it won't be Inaba's."

It was both a warning and a question.

Reik grimaced. He didn't have to explain how he was pulled in both directions. He'd spent his life trying to balance on a knife's edge and his friend knew it. "I hope to stick to our original plan and avoid the choice."

Daisuke just sighed—then glanced around. "Then what are we doing out here, dude?"

"You are giving me a ride, I hope—and then hauling snake butt out of here."

Daisuke's tail hissed in protest, but he just laughed. "My butt is *tanuki*, not snake, as you well know." He sobered. "So where am I taking you? And what will you be doing there?"

Reik gestured toward the peak above. "There. Where I'll be righting an old wrong."

"How old?" his friend asked knowingly.

He met his gaze. "About as old as me."

Daisuke sighed. "You're sure you want to do this?"

He nodded.

"All right, then."

"I need to be stealthy," Reik told him. "Do you think you could carry me and give us the cover of one of your dark clouds, too?" Transformation and travel as a black cloud was a Nue trait—and more than once Daisuke had avoided confrontation just with the eerie sound of his battle cry echoing from the sky. The spine-tingling combination had sent more than one potential opponent running before actual combat could begin.

Daisuke bared monkey teeth. "Yeesh. I don't know. I generally phase out when I go that route . . ." He frowned, clearly thinking. "But we can give it a shot."

"I appreciate it, my friend," Reik said quietly.

"Yeah, let's get it done first, before you get sappy." Daisuke was still frowning. "Where are we going? Give me a route to follow. I doubt you'll be able to see, if this works."

Reik explained and described both the path he'd taken down the mountain and the clearing with the cave. Daisuke listened, nodded, then jerked his head. "Go ahead and climb on my back. I'll try to phase out just enough to generate a cover."

"Let me get my things." Reik pulled his pack out of the igloo and strapped it on. "Okay. Let's do this." He climbed aboard Daisuke's broad, furry back—the thick barrel of a Japanese raccoon dog or *tanuki*. He dug his fingers into the soft fur. "Ready."

"Give me a minute. I have to see if I can partially phase without dropping you . . ."

Nothing happened for a time. Suddenly Reik looked down as smoke-colored vapor began to flow out from underneath them.

"Hold on," Daisuke said, his voice strained. Crouching, he launched them upwards. Reik tightened his hold on the fur in front of him and recoiled a little as he sank into his seat. Literally. "Ah, yeah—this is awkward!" he called as he passed a little way through his friend's suddenly less substantial form.

"It's not so great from down here, either," Daisuke answered testily. "And this cloud cover is going to be small and not very natural looking, I'm guessing. But it's the best I can do."

Reik was in no position to criticize. They rose higher and the world around them began to fade as the cloud grew thicker.

"I'm going to keep low, just above the tree level."

"Yeah. Stop outside the clearing too, so we can scope it out."

They moved slowly and steadily up the mountain. Though he was quickly unable to see beyond the cloud, the normal sounds of the wilderness continued on around them, reassuring Reik that they must be mostly disguised.

"Okay," Daisuke said after a bit. "I think this is it. I'm going to hover here a moment."

Reik had been thinking. "Can you get me in close to a tree? A fir tree?"

"Yeah."

Slowly they edged sideways. Through the dark mist first

emerged the branches and then the trunk of an evergreen. Reik leaned in and snatched a lap full of cones. "Can you sense anything?" he asked his friend. "I'm blind as a bat in here."

"Nothing," Daisuke answered after a moment. "I think the place is empty."

"Okay. Let's move in. Can you drop down right in front of the cave? Just get low—I don't want you to land. I've already tripped more than one of his booby traps."

Reik felt his friend's shoulders lift. "Are you sure you want to do this?"

"Yes. I just don't want you to get mixed up in it."

Daisuke sighed. "All right."

Reik felt it when they began to descend. "Are we close enough for me to get down?"

"Yeah."

"Hear anything? Sense anything?"

"Nope. Nothing. I don't think anyone is home."

"Okay. Get ready," he warned. "I'm going to drop a couple of cones first."

He tossed a pinecone over onto the fresh snow below.

Nothing.

He dropped a few more, in other directions. No reaction. Slowly, he relaxed. "All right, then. I'm going in." He shifted his weight and pointed a toe towards the ground. "If something happens, shoot for the sky. I'll hang on."

Gradually, he set one foot on the ground, shifting all of his weight slowly. His other foot slid over and he stood carefully, waiting.

They had set down several steps away from the mouth of the cave. Reik gave a little jump. Nothing. He grinned hugely up at Daisuke. "You did it! Thank you."

The Nue hovered and stared at the cave entrance. "What's in there?"

Reik followed his gaze. "Part of my past. Hope for a better future. And trouble. Definitely trouble." He bounced again. "Daisuke?"

His friend glanced down at him.

"Thanks for getting me here." He let his gaze confer all the gratitude and camaraderie that he couldn't say out loud. "But you should go."

"You're sure you don't want me to wait?"

"No." He looked again to the cave. "This is something I have to do alone."

The monkey face looked skeptical.

"I'll come for you after it's done, eh?" Reik offered. "And maybe we'll come up with a spot out of the way . . . where we can stay out of bigger trouble?"

That barreled chest swelled with a sigh. "It was a nice idea, my friend, but I'm afraid it's a pipe dream."

"Yes, well—It seemed a dream that a scout from Ryu and a Nue could be friends, didn't it?" He waved a hand toward the cave. "And I've been dreaming of this almost my whole life— and here I am."

Daisuke nodded thoughtfully. "Maybe you're right. Tell you what, do you remember when we camped by that lake and stole a barrel of sake from those shōjō?"

Reik laughed. "I'll not soon forget that headache."

"I'll wait for you there. Find me when you've taken care of this business."

He nodded and watched while Daisuke faded away, phasing completely into his dark cloud form and rising high above the ridge. He waved and the cloud drifted away.

His heart in his throat, Reik turned to the cave. He'd waited long enough. It was time to begin—and to set his mother free.

# CHAPTER 5

R eik walked the last few feet to the cave's entrance, pausing at the curved rock to listen. Not a sound or a breath of air stirred from the darkness. He placed a hand on the rock and glanced behind him. No sign of . . . anything. Taking a breath, he took the step that would take him inside.

Correction. Tried to take a step. His foot was caught . . .

He looked down to find ice creeping up from the ground, inching up and around both of his feet.

His heart rate ratcheted up, but he merely waved a couple of fingers to disperse it.

The ice continued, covering his feet and creeping up towards his ankles.

Muttering a curse, he jerked his hand in command.

The ice didn't obey.

He blinked. How was that possible? He tried harder to lift one foot, then the other. He tried to kick out. Attempted to jump with both feet at once.

He was caught—and the ice was still growing. It spread, reaching between his feet and connecting them, adding layers beneath him, not stopping until his feet were encases in an odd shaped block that curved on the bottom and up the sides.

"What in all of the ancient kingdoms?" He looked up, but Daisuke was long gone.

And whatever enchantment Runar had set into motion hadn't finished yet. The snow beneath his encased feet began to transform. It moved, hollowed and hardened, making a trench that fit the curved block that held him fast. Reik crouched down—and realized the trench was extending behind him.

He quickly stood again, wind-milled his arms to keep his balance, and looked over his shoulder. His gut clenched as he realized it wasn't a trench—it was a *track*—and it was growing longer, stretching out behind him.

"Oh, no," he whispered, and tried to stand perfectly still.

It didn't matter. Runar clearly had had something specific in mind. With a small, scraping sound, the block of ice at his feet began to shift backwards—taking him with it.

It moved slowly at first as it dragged him back across the clearing. When it hit the forest slope beyond, it began to pick up speed. Reik reached desperately for branches, trunks, anything he whipped past, but the pull was relentless and he couldn't hold on for long. Forced to let go of a long, thick branch, he struggled, off balance. But the ice climbed up his calves and steadied him.

He bit his lip, stifling the urge to shout his frustration. No need to attract Runar's attention, if he could help it. He still might get out of this—whatever this turned out to be in the end.

Down he went, undulating over the forest floor, until at last the track hit a frozen pond. It carried him out onto the ice, slowing as it went and stopping when he ground to a halt in the middle of the pond.

A glance over his shoulder told him the track ended here. He glared around, twisting to see all sides, but he was alone.

He breathed deep, waiting, forcing himself to remain calm.

No one came. No sign of Runar or White Shoulders. Just the creak of tree branches in the cold breeze.

He stifled anger, panic and impatience and reached for calm. Closing his eyes, he took a moment to take stock.

Okay, then. He breathed deeply. Opening his eyes, he looked into the sky and called for snow.

Relief snaked through his veins when the clouds above him thickened and fat flakes began to fall. Yes. Good. He wasn't completely powerless.

Sucking in a deep breath, he tried again with the ice holding his feet, but again, there was no response there. The pond was frozen through. Reik tried to make contact with the ice below, but it was deaf to him as well.

Well, then.

He concentrated then, and called his own ice, forming it between his hands and manufacturing a tool—with a sharp pick on one end and bent crow bar on the other. He went to work on the block around his feet, trying to chip or pry his way out. But the ice was impervious no matter what tactic he tried—even to the hard, hammering, frustrated blows he ended with.

Eventually, he stopped, and slumped, exhausted, to the ground. He scooted his back end up close to his bent knees and laid back, arms spread, still clutching his ice pick, and stared at the sky.

The snow fell on. He blinked up at it as it caught in his lashes. This was it, then. Runar would deign to come and find him sometime—and he would be forced to enter into their confrontation at a serious disadvantage.

He sighed and closed his eyes against the assault of the

snowflakes, feeling their soft touch on his face. Time passed. He drifted in and out. Not asleep, but not truly awake, either. Adrift.

Suddenly he opened his eyes and the snow had been replaced with whirling colors. The snow globe. He felt a touch on his arm and looked over to find his mother beside him.

He forgot, sometimes, how beautiful she was. Delicate features and creamy skin—and an expression that gave nothing away. She took his hand and waved the other toward the landscape below. It was the same small village he'd seen in his last dream, but this time they'd come at night. Everything lay still and quiet, covered with the sparkle of moonlight reflecting on a light snow cover.

His mother swooped downward, pulling him with her. Her ebony hair flowed back, contrasting with her rich, white robes. She floated over the ground, and he did too, as long as she held him. She dropped down, aiming for a small cottage on the edge of the village, stopping at the door and letting him go.

She let herself in. Reluctantly, he followed. It was little more than a hut, just two rooms. The smaller one contained an elderly couple, asleep on thin pallets on the floor. Yuki Onna took a step toward the old man, her kimono gleaming in the dark. Reik closed his eyes against what he knew would happen next.

His mother was *yokai*. The Snow Woman. She survived by draining others of their chi, their life force. Since Inaba had experimented on her, she sometimes drained mortals of blood too. Reik didn't know which she intended to do to this man, but he could stomach neither.

"Come, mother." He had to try. "Let's go and leave these people in peace."

She looked at him without blinking, without any obvious

reaction. Then her gaze slid to the old man again. She moved closer.

Reik stepped in front of her, trying to block her way.

Her beautiful face did not change. It didn't register anger or sorrow or even annoyance at his interference. She just stepped around him, intent on her victim, her hunger, as if his plea didn't touch her at all.

He didn't want any part of it. He turned away as she knelt over the old man, but she suddenly moved, reaching for him and clamping a cold hand over his wrist.

He stiffened—and suddenly understood something he hadn't before. His mother drained the man's chi—and as she did, images danced across her vision—and somehow she was sharing them. They were all there, the important moments of the old man's life—births and deaths, laughter and loves, quiet times of gratitude and repose, battles, big and small. He stared, mesmerized, until the images slowed—and the old man weakened.

Reik pulled away and his mother released the man. He lay still on his pallet, his breathing shallow, but he was still alive. Reik turned and walked out of the cottage.

His mother followed. She stared at him, intense and looking as if she wanted him to understand something.

A noise sounded before she could say anything. A throat clearing.

They both jumped. Yuki Onna frowned and looked to the side—

And Reik woke up.

# CHAPTER 6

It sounded again, that throat clearing noise, and Reik blinked his eyes open. Frowning, he blinked several times more.

A face stared down at him. A mature face, broad and brown and wrinkled in the best way—as if smiles and laughter had left their mark upon flesh.

But this face—and the woman attached to it—was more than flesh. The spirit-born part of his soul reared up in recognition to the creature standing over him.

All of this flashed through his head in an instant. Then the woman raised her brows. "What's this, then?" she asked.

Instant awareness stabbed through him. "Oh, no," he gasped, sitting up. Shards—he'd forgotten his feet were still frozen. He looked around, a bit on the frantic side. "You've got to get out of here. Hurry! It's not safe."

She'd withdrawn a fraction as he sat up. She looked like a woman of one of the local Native American tribes. Puyallup? Nisqually? She wore a parka of fur, intricately designed in patterns of different pelts. He huffed out a breath. It didn't matter. "You have to go."

"Why?" She sounded unconcerned.

"A man . . . a creature . . ." Reik scanned the area around the pond again. "He's . . . He's dangerous. You should go."

She gestured toward his feet. "He did this?"

"Yes, you don't want him to get hold of you."

Nodding, she lifted a pack to her shoulder.

"Wait!" The pack looked heavy. "Are you carrying . . .?" He gestured from her pack to her feet. "Do you have any tools that could help me?"

"You speak of the ice mage, yes?"

At his slow nod, her head tilted. "If this is his work, then there is no mortal tool that will help you."

His heart sank. "Who are you?"

"I put the same question to you. Who are you to the creature you speak of—the one who seeks power, here on the mountain?"

"I'm . . . nothing." He gave a dark laugh. "His next meal, perhaps."

She gave a sniff of disgust. "You would lie to an old woman?"

Shaking his head, he let it drop onto his knee. "Just go, before you get hurt."

When he looked up, several minutes later, she was still there. Her gaze shone steady and measuring.

"You want to be free, yes?" she asked.

He sat up straight. "Yes."

"Then tell me why you have come to this place."

Reik flopped onto his back again. The snow had stopped falling, he noticed idly.

"Why?" she repeated.

He sighed. "I just want to help my mother." It came out on a whisper.

She didn't respond. After a moment, he turned his head to find her looking at him with narrowed eyes.

Her stare made him feel vulnerable. Transparent. As if she could see through to his soul.

She gave an abrupt, brisk nod and walked away.

He swallowed bitter disappointment.

Reaching the edge of the pond, she stepped up onto the bank. Turning, she lifted a shoulder in question. "Well? Are you coming?"

He pointed with both index fingers at his trapped feet. "Uh, no?"

"Oh, yes." She pointed her finger too, and the encasing ice melted down his calves and past his ankles and on until the soles of his boots were free.

His mouth dropped and he sprang onto his feet just as an ominous crack sounded. Just like that, all the ice in the pond melted.

He dropped down into the depths.

Sputtering and kicking, he tried to swim back up, but his pack weighed him down. With a mental curse, he slid out of it and surfaced. "How did you do that?" he called. The water wasn't even cold. Even a full-blooded human would have been comfortable in it.

"Come on, then," she ordered. She turned away. "We'd better get you dry."

Reik kicked, treading water for a moment, and then he gave a mental shrug and swam for the edge.

DRIPPING WATER, Reik hurried to catch up. He had to work at it. This *yokai* moved quickly, for all that she held the form of an older woman.

"Hey," he called as he finally caught her. "Are you going to tell me who you are? And how you did that?" He waved a hand down his sodden form, doubly thankful at this moment, that the cold didn't affect him and doubly curious about her identity. There were some *yokai* who held mastery over elements, like the wind demon who had hunted his friend Mei for so long. Those beings were few and far between, however, and usually extremely powerful.

"Yes." She didn't pause or look back. "But not now. You were right about one thing. The ice mage is coming for you."

Involuntarily, he glanced back over his shoulder.

"We'll talk once we have you safe."

He didn't argue, just used his breath to keep pace with her. They covered a good bit of ground, moving through thick forest, and keeping to roughly the same altitude, as far as he could tell. When the forest thinned and he could see across the range of smaller peaks below, he checked the sun and thought they were facing south and east.

The ground grew rockier. They came to a drop and turned to follow the edge. Reik realized it was a ridge similar to the one that contained Runar's cave. It lacked the clearing and the ice flow, but it boasted a sharp turn at the top and a descent that appeared almost stair-like—and worn from long use.

They stepped down into a curious space, long and formed by the ridge wall on one side and a long row of jagged boulders on the other. Ahead, the line of boulders angled in to meet the wall, leaving a triangular space between, open and hidden from the outside.

"Goats," his companion said, gesturing to a small, covered pen near the apex of the triangle.

But Reik's attention was not on the empty pen or the barrels stacked alongside it. His focus was entirely riveted on the opening in the ridge wall. Oblong, it stretched wide but stood only slightly taller than him. It angled back into the mountain. A chill went down his spine as he recognized what it was. "A lava tube."

"Yes." She moved to stand before the opening. "I am willing to be your friend, child. But friendship goes two ways. Will you pledge yours? Will you act in the ways of truth and trust and the sharing of goodwill?"

He looked into her broad, weathered face and saw kindness shine from her dark eyes. Still, he hesitated. What she offered was simple, but also profound. He was not used to openness. He hid much of himself, even from those he called friends.

But this strange, lone woman stirred up an old longing in him. What a relief it would be to have someone to listen, to know.

She meant what she said. She offered him friendship. He could feel her sincerity. What he wanted, with a sudden fierceness, was her understanding.

"I . . ." He squeezed his eyes shut, then opened them, speaking quickly. "I will." He held out a hand. "I could use a friend."

She clasped his arm, reaching nearly to his elbow. "Everyone benefits from the blessings of true friendship." Stepping aside, she waved him in. "Welcome to my home."

Moving slowly, he followed the tunnel-like entrance into the depths of the mountain. After several feet, the narrow passage opened up.

The ceiling rose higher here, creating an open, round-ish living space. It was all done up in neutral colors, in rugs of natural fibers, cedar furniture and a good number of oil lamps that all lit simultaneously with a wave of his hostess's hand. The air felt comfortable and warm, a fact that unnerved him a little, considering the nature and origin of the place.

He shifted. It felt disrespectful to be standing wet and still dripping a little, in her cozy abode. But he had to know. "Who are you?"

She tossed him a towel. "I have many names," she answered, shrugging. "You may call me Tak'homa."

He stilled. His duties as a scout had sent him to the Seattle area a couple of time before. It was how he'd met Daisuke, in fact, on a journey up the coast from JanFran. Like any good scout, he'd studied up on the legends of the area he was entering. Her name was familiar. More than the name of the city south of here—it was also the Native American name for this volcanic mountain.

Had he just befriended the spirit of the mountain? A creature that must be eons old and more powerful than he could imagine?

He suddenly wished he could sit down.

"What is your name, child?"

"Reik," he answered wearily.

"Well, Reik. As at least part of you is human—I imagine you are tired and hungry. Let's get you comfortable first, eh?"

He could only nod and follow as she led him to the back of the main room, where two tunnels branched off in opposite directions. Numb, he followed her directions around the curved passage to the bathroom. Modern facilities lay tucked away, and a huge bathing pool hewn from rock. It ran with a current of warm, flowing water.

He soaked a long time, letting the heat ease tense muscles and fog the worry in his brain. When he emerged, his own clothes were gone. He donned the replacements and Tak'homa met him as he shuffled back toward the main room.

Her measuring eye roved over him before she gave a sharp nod. "Rest first," she said firmly. She pointed toward the opposite curving hallway. "First room on the right. Sleep yourself out. I will be here."

～

REIK FELL onto a thick pallet covered in furs and slept. And slept. For long, dreamless hours. The most restful sleep he'd had—perhaps ever. Eventually, though, he awoke and stretched, unsure what time or day it was, and reluctant to find out.

Boneless, he lay there, going over the past few days in his mind. The worry tried to push back in. Had he made a mistake? What did Tak'homa know of him—of his background? Of his family? Would she thwart him if she knew? Or could she help him in his mission?

He pushed the roiling thoughts away, rolled over and drifted back to sleep.

A mistake, perhaps.

He dreamed this time. His mother again led him across an ancient, Japanese landscape. It occurred to him, as they passed towns and mills, fields and villages and country inns, that he should be paying attention, taking notes. Was this a glimpse into the true past? Was he witnessing an utterly unique view of a culture nearly wiped from the earth?

But his mother demanded his focus. She let him see . . . everything. Things he didn't wish to, certainly. The paths she had tread upon, a *yokai* following winter's borders as they expanded and shrank and expanded again with the seasons. She showed him the lives she'd taken and some she had spared. He saw them die, saw them realize that the beautiful girl they'd found lost in the cold mountain passes would be their doom. He saw her follow travelers home to their villages and watched them take her in. Sometimes she would stay, struck by a sudden fancy for a pretty youth, or a lively mind, and live with a man as his wife. She would seem content, too, for a time, but something always happened to give her away and she would fade into the mist, disappear, never to be seen again. And another legend of Yuki Onna, the Snow Woman, would be born.

Abruptly and without warning, the dream disappeared, like someone had turned off a vid monitor in his head.

He stirred and sat up to find Tak'homa standing in the open doorway. "That's enough of that," she said dryly. Turning, she beckoned. "Time to eat."

He followed.

"Come." She called him from the kitchen alcove attached to the main room. A hearth with a small fire burning was the central focus. There were also rock-hewn containers and shelves and an assortment of stacked earthenware and hand woven baskets.

"Sit." Tak'homa indicated one of the cushions on the floor and crossed to the fire.

He sank down, noting for the first time, the texture of his borrowed clothes. He rubbed a finger over a soft fold of tunic and lifted it to inhale deeply. "Cedar bark?" he asked in wonder.

Looking over her shoulder, the spirit nodded.

"It's so much softer than I thought it would be." He studied the fit. It was a close match, although the pant legs were a little long on him. A memory broke free. "You have a son, yes? These are his?"

"I do." She knelt, handing him a covered bowl and took the other cushion. "Tahoma. He has his own home, not far away, but I keep a few things here."

He stilled. Little Tahoma Peak—a satellite of Mount Rainier, quite visible from Seattle. Someone had told him the story. Long ago the spirits of the mountains had lived as people. In the crowded mountain ranges a man had lived with two wives, who had quarreled bitterly with each other. Exasperated when her husband refused to intervene, Tak'homa had taken her son and moved on, traveling to a more open plain. With more room and good living, they had grown and grown, in size and strength.

"It's true, then? You are the spirit of this mountain?"

She nodded. Leaning over, she lifted the lid from his bowl. "Eat."

Despite his unease, his stomach growled. Salmon and rice and some sort of baked gourd. It smelled divine and tasted better. He ate steadily, watching her as he did.

She looked so . . . normal. Human. She watched him, too, obviously enjoying his pleasure in the food. Nothing about her easy, wrinkled visage spoke of power. She could have been anyone's grandmother, happy to welcome a friend with warmth and hospitality.

"Was my—" He stopped, struck suddenly. "Was the ice mage chanting to *you*? When he performed that ritual the other day?"

Tak'homa took a last few, slow bites. Setting her bowl down, she nodded.

"Why?" he asked. "What did it mean?"

She waved a hand. "It's just another attempt to get my attention."

Reik frowned. "He comes here, to your mountain, every winter?"

"For the last several years," she said with a nod.

"Why?"

"Because he wants . . . more, as best as I have been able to figure."

"More? More of . . . what?"

"More of everything. Everything he has a surfeit of already. More of everything he doesn't need." She frowned. "But I've watched him carefully. Listened to the songs in his heart." He head shook. "He'll be getting nothing from me, no matter what sorts of antics he gets up to."

He tried to imagine Runar's reaction on hearing that.

"Enough of him. He doesn't interest me." She leaned in. "You, on the other hand, do."

Reik had no idea how to respond.

"I knew the moment you stepped on the mountain, of course."

Tone was everything, in this conversation. The words might have sounded menacing, coming from someone else. But there was no tension in her, only a certain curiosity in her voice.

"Many humans come to the mountain, in all seasons. I ignore them, for the most part. But you—the echo of your father's magic sings in your blood. And more besides." She met his gaze directly. "Let us talk of your mother."

Reik stiffened. All of his defenses slammed back up. "I hardly have anything to say of her."

He never spoke of his mother. She was his secret. His mission. She was just . . . his.

Tak'homa straightened. Her gaze wandered over him, slow and measuring. "I see. And yet you said you wished to help her, when I asked why you came to the mountain."

He stared into the fire and said nothing.

"Reik, does your father have some hold over her?" The question emerged gently, floating between them like a thistle on the wind.

He considered the ramifications of answering even that. And the possible consequences of *not* answering.

He sighed and nodded.

Tak'homa frowned. "The ice mage is many times more powerful than you are. You cannot defeat him."

His jaw tightened. "I don't have to defeat him. I need only to get what I came for and get away."

"I'm not sure it can be done. He'll likely kill you."

"I am not completely defenseless," he objected.

She shook her head, her bright gaze dimming with sadness. "You might as well be a swaddled babe. He has lived long and longer and collected more than one kind of magic."

Reik refused to give in to the slump that tugged at his shoulders. It didn't matter that he wasn't strong enough. The war was coming, as everyone insisted on reminding him. Inaba's plans were coming to fruition and his mother would play a part in them. A dangerous part, it was likely, if the rumors were true and Yuki Onna had lost her master's favor. He had to free her before the battles began.

"It may be that I can help you," Tak'homa said suddenly. She climbed to her feet. "I will walk and think on it. Would you care to join me?"

Unexpected hope surged. "Yes." She would help him? He would take it—anything she could give. "Yes, I would."

CHAPTER 7

L ight from the late afternoon sun spread warm colors
across the snow. He must have slept most of the day
away. Tak'homa handed him a tunic of light fur. He didn't
need it, but as she paused atop the jumbled row of boulders
outside her home, he donned it anyway. Nimbly, she hopped
down and set out into the woods.

He followed. It was no hardship, for she was in no hurry
this time. Cold and quiet, the scrubby forest seemed to be
edging toward sleep, the soft breeze a sigh of tired content-
ment. Except, that is, where Tak'homa went. When she
stepped into a glade or strode through a clearing, there was a
stirring, a quiet awakening, and greetings.

Birds swooped down to hover before her or to perch on
an outstretched arm. They chirped companionably to her,
reminding him strongly of his friend and nemesis, Ken Sato.
Just as Ken did, the mountain spirit listened, head cocked
and attentive, nodding as if in understanding.

She touched things as she walked. A brush of fingers
along an outcropping of rock. A pause while she stood, hand
splayed across the heart of a tree. Once she stopped and

plunged both hands into a fast-moving stream. The shadows had begun to stretch out as the sun lowered, but Reik swore he saw . . . something . . . rise up from the depths and brush across her fingers.

Cool mist began to arise. It swirled at their feet and surrounded an extended stretch of rock as she climbed up onto it. It circled her as she settled into a sitting position and stared out and he wondered if she could see through it.

He took up a position at the base of the outcropping, keeping to his feet. "You are connected to it, aren't you?" he asked quietly. "All of it."

"Yes. The mountain is part of me, just as I am part of it. All of the life here, the soil, the wind, the rock beneath us and the fire that lives below. We are many. And we are one."

He marveled at the idea, even as he found it uncomfortable.

She turned a bit so that she could see him. "You are very young," she said, grinning.

"A blink of an eye, compared to you, I am sure. But I'm not flattering you when I say that you don't *feel* like you are as old as you surely must be."

"I thank you." She twinkled at him. "There must, of course, be many differences between us, but I think there are similarities as well."

"You think so?"

"Stubbornness, perhaps," she said with a laugh. "A bit of cynicism?"

"I'll own up to both of those."

She sighed. "Love, too. Love is love at any age and I sense the feelings you carry for your mother." Spreading her fingers wide, she waved a hand and the mist swirled away. Below them stretched a long, snow-covered slope and beyond the edge of it rose a pyramid of striated rock. "My son sleeps there. He has been asleep for some time."

The peak looked far more intimidating up close than it did from the city. "When will he awake?"

"Perhaps in the spring. Perhaps next spring. It has always been his favorite season." Her wrinkled face broadened into a grimace. "I envy him, sometimes. Especially on nights like this, when it seems all the world welcomes the soft night. It has been some time since I slept."

"Why?" Was it because of his father?

"These are not restful times. I keep watch."

He could not fault her thinking. He wondered if she knew what had happened to the volcanic peak south of here.

"Though I am occasionally weary, I take on the duty willingly. I have grown stronger than my son, over the years, and so I allow him to rest and gather his strength."

"There are some who would reverse that. Use their power to force the job on him—because they could."

"Yes. Some would. I am glad you see the difference, young one. I protect my son, would do anything for him, because of the love I feel for him. His feelings toward me are the same." She speared him with a direct look. "Is that how things are with your mother?"

He nodded.

"Real, abiding love must be given freely, my son. It cannot flourish where there is coercion."

He nodded again, not sure what she meant to say beneath her words.

"It is this way with you? You are under no compulsion?"

"From my mother?" he asked, finally understanding. "No," he answered somewhat bitterly. "No. If there is any hint of . . . darkness . . . in our connection, it must surely come from me."

His answer troubled her, he could see. "Are you sure?"

"Yes. My mother is coerced. I am not."

Sitting back, she nodded. "Very well, then." The mist had

51

come creeping back. A tendril curled up and over her shoulder, looking for all the world like it was peeking at him. "Tomorrow, we will begin."

~

NOT SURPRISINGLY, he dreamed of his mother that night.

Almost as soon as he lay down, he fell asleep, and found her waiting. She pulled him down into the world of the snow globe, the world of her past. She still did not speak, but he could read the urgency in her manner.

She took him straight to a cold evening on a frost-covered road, where she followed a caravan of traders. As the night came on, they rolled into a sizable, crossroads village and sought lodging for the night.

She had her eye on a particular young man, strapping and good-humored. But as she crept into the roadside inn that night, Reik saw the moment that something else caught her attention.

One moment she was moving along a back passage in the crowded back of the inn and the next she was looking up, her head turned toward the stairs that led to the more luxurious rooms, her usually calm expression alight with curiosity—and hunger.

He followed as she moved without touching the floor. She crept to the top of the inn, passed several doors and stopped at one at the end of a decorated hallway. Inside open trunks were pushed against a wall, next to a fine leather saddle. A girl's robes lay strewn across the floor. No girl was in sight, though. The only occupant was a man, asleep and covered in richly embroidered blankets.

Yuki Onna approached him with evident eagerness. She stood over him, hands extended and shaking a little, eyes closed. Reik stared. She looked so different. Always before she fed with a matter-of-fact approach. Just another necessity. Yet now her flat, calm manner had given way to appetite and anticipation.

The man rolled over. He slept on, right through Reik's gasp of recognition and his bark of warning and alarm.

Inaba.

Reik's stomach turned. The features were unmistakable, even though he looked warm, flush with color and life compared to the cool, grey blue tones of his appearance in Reik's time. The cruelty was still there, though, apparent in his features even at rest.

Reik reached for his mother, cried out for her to turn away, to *run*.

But she was caught. Enraptured by something—something in his energy? In his life force? Clearly some part of him called to her. And she answered, bending to drink of his chi even as Reik awoke with a shout on his lips and the heavy press of doom in his heart.

Sleep was a long time coming afterward, and it felt as if morning arrived just as soon as he'd dropped into an exhausted rest. But Tak'homa was knocking at his door and standing in the frame, beckoning.

"Let's begin," she ordered. "There is much to learn and none of it is easy."

CHAPTER 8

*Spirits, monsters and ancestors*, but truer words were never spoken.

Tak'homa took him out onto a snow-covered meadow and put him through his paces. She asked him to show her his every skill and trick. Walls and spikes and thin, dangerous sheets of ice. Sleet, freezing rain and fat, fluffy snow. Hoarfrost and hollow columns and high flying, razor-sharp discs.

She asked question after question, wanting to know everything about how he manipulated the ice, how he called it, how he felt connected to it. She wanted to know when his talents first manifested, which skills came first, and which required the most effort to master.

Pure torture. Every bit of it. Reik had always been very careful to hide his full range of abilities. He never shared any personal information if he could avoid it. He'd never discussed *any* of this with anyone. He doubted even his mother knew this much about him.

But he gritted his teeth and answered the mountain spirit's questions. He performed like a trick pony. He ignored all of his usual barriers and laid himself bare before her.

Her almost clinical manner made it all a little easier. A nod, a quiet word of praise or a thoughtful frown was the extent of her reactions. And the coaching she began to give on the second day made it easier, still.

She lectured him about weather conditions, made him sit and listen to her talk of humidity and differences between water and vapor, and soil and air temperature—and how they all could be used, adjusted and adapted for. Best of all, she taught him new and unusual skills for different conditions.

"It's easier for me," she told him. "I can command more than one element at once. But you can adjust your attacks according to your environment. For example, if I warm the frozen earth and ensure the soil is just slightly warmer than the air . . ." She gestured toward a slip of land near a streambed. "There. There is water beneath the soil. Can you feel it?"

He nodded. He could usually feel the presence of water, in all of its forms.

"It is nearly frozen, but not quite. Will it respond to you?" she asked. "Call it."

He did—and tiny, translucent, sharp pikes sprouted from the ground.

"Needle ice," she said. "Now, imagine if there was more water available beneath the surface."

He could feel it move in as she directed it. It was cold—on the verge of freezing. He called—and this time great, shining spikes erupted from the ground.

"That could be useful," he said, nodding.

She took him back to the pond, which had frozen once more. She thawed it and taught him to cover the surface with deadly sharp, eerily beautiful frost flowers. "The water must be dead calm and the air significantly colder than the ice over the water," she told him. "It's much easier in sea water, where the salinity is higher."

He filed it all away, and thanked her repeatedly for the instruction.

"I imagine you could go through your life just freezing your opponents solid and shattering them into pieces," she said in response, one day. "But there is strength and structure in the make up of ice. You can use it to build and create. Ice can be sustaining and preserving. I'm willing to bet that with training and effort, you could even learn to heal or to augment a life force." She looked solemn. "The day is coming when you will have to choose your path."

She gave him much to think about and she often sat him on a rock in the sun and had him meditate. She asked him to look deep inside himself and to find the energy center that connected him with his element. She taught him to nurture it, to strengthen and widen the bond he felt.

And it worked. His *minding* talents were stretching, growing. The ice responded more quickly and more easily shaped itself to his will.

It was thrilling. Exhilarating. And it was damned exhausting work.

Tak'homa seemed to understand this, too. When they had finished a long day's work, she would take him back to her home—and spoil him.

There really was no other word for it. She cooked him nourishing meals and supplied fresh and clean clothes. One morning he woke and his pack was in his room, dry and like it had never sat on the bottom of the icy pond. She offered him free reign of her small collection of books. But despite several intriguing titles, he was too tired to take advantage of the kindness.

Fortunately, she sensed when he'd had more than enough

interaction and left him alone when he needed it. On other nights, she sat companionably with him in the main room of her home, sharing old folk tales and stories from her long life.

He felt a twinge now and then, an urge to share stories of his own. To tell her of his friends. About wise Sho. And fierce Hitomi, whose *minding* talent was a form of shape shifting, but whose heart was an even more powerful weapon. About Ken who was like a brother and also a thorn in his side. And Mei. That pretty girl, both incredibly strong and infinitely fragile. The Girl With the Stars in Her Eyes, the one the prophecies had long spoke of. The one who would face Inaba, in the end.

But he fought the urge to talk of them. He held his feelings for them close, safe from exposure, from manipulation. From acknowledgement, if hard truths must be told.

Still, despite his own miserly temperament, Tak'homa's kindness humbled him. This ancient and powerful spirit treated him . . . like a son.

Acknowledging it set loose a whirlwind of conflicting emotion in his gut. Part of him felt he didn't deserve it. Part of him relished it all. This was the stuff of his fantasies—his childhood dreams that had taken root and motivated him to this day. Motherly care, interest and instruction—he had longed for it all.

But Tak'homa was not his mother and he felt like a traitor.

These were all the things he'd been hoping to find with Yuki Onna once she was freed from Runar's hold and Inaba's influence. It felt wrong to experience it with someone else. Especially as his nights were still filled with dreams of his mother and the disturbing tale of how she'd come to be trapped.

Night after night, Reik watched helplessly. Inaba's energy appeared to be a drug that Yuki Onna could not resist. In the dreams, she followed the young lord on his travels, and because she shared the images she saw as she siphoned off his chi, Reik began to understand why.

Inaba's life story played out in incredibly different ways from the tales of his mother's usual victims. Scenes from his childhood showed a pampered life of the son of a daimyo, and yet, his family appeared to disdain him. Dinners were lively family affairs, but he sat silent and sullen. The boys trained every day, learning archery and swordplay and poetry like every Samurai's son, but Inaba's skills appeared to lag behind, his efforts looked half-hearted at best. His brother appeared to torment him, his father's gaze passed over him. His mother watched and scolded, sniffed in disdain and shook her head in disappointment.

Why?

He could not tell, from the silent images his mother shared. But they both watched as, in the face of his family's hostility, the young Inaba wandered down rare and dark paths. Reik thought those experiences must lend him the qualities that called to Yuki Onna. The scenes that played out while she fed were filled with dank caves and ancient magic, dark witchcraft and disturbing spells. He chased after those rumored to have magic and pursued objects reported to transfer strange gifts to their owners. Even Reik could feel that his energy began to warp as he explored sinister enchantments and twisted sources of power.

As his strength grew and he cut a swath through the known magicians in the realm, Inaba began to turn his eye to other sources. He sought to bargain with *kami* for spiritual energy. And he turned to *yokai*, as well. He spent an inordinate amount of effort trying to catch a mermaid-like Ningyo, whose consumed flesh was rumored to grant immortal life. And he began to search for ways to capture *yokai* and bend them to his will.

Reik could see where this was going, even if it appeared as if Yuki Onna did not. He pleaded with her to turn away and let Inaba go, but she was locked on this path. She even left the cold north to follow him to the city of Edo, where her powers weakened in the warmer climate.

He watched with dread. Why could his mother not see what was happening? What was coming?

It did come, then, just as Reik feared. He stared one night while his mother, grown too eager and careless, entered Inaba's luxurious rooms at his family's Edo palace. She bent over his slumbering form, as always—except this time, the white and glowing flow of chi between them turned suddenly blood red.

Reik gasped.

His mother froze.

Inaba's eyes opened.

The red color spread over Yuki Onna, trapping her in place. It spread over Inaba too, as he sat up and stared at the Snow Woman. The red-tinged crackle of energy still connected them. Did he know that she'd been stalking him for weeks? Siphoning off his life force and re-living the story of his life?

Inaba bent low to examine her. He muttered under his breath as he stood up and circled her. And then he threw back his head and laughed.

"No," Reik groaned in the dream. "No!"

Inaba's head cocked. He looked in Reik's direction—

And Reik jerked awake, back in his bed, with Tak'homa once again standing over him. She had a hand on his chest and a frown on her face.

"No more." She shook her head. "Come. Your father is causing trouble."

"This part of the mountain is shielded," she said as she led him out of her cave and up the rough steps to the ridge above. "At the edges of my own space, I can bend the light, manipulate the shadows, disguise the way and fool the eye, urging intruders to move away from my own private territory. It's worked for hundreds of years—on your father, too." She shrugged as she looked back at him. "I don't know what has changed. He might be scenting you. Or he might be able to sense you in other ways. But he's found a way in."

She was leading him toward the meadow they'd practiced in yesterday. She'd had him manufacturing tiny, thin ice darts and throwing them in rapid succession to pin her tunic to a tree—without piercing her flesh. It had taken a deal of practice to perfect the uniformity of the darts and the precision of his aim. And though he'd avoided spearing Tak'homa, he had worried a bit for the health of the tree behind her.

He could have spared the concern. The tree—and a dozen others spaced around the meadow—had been ripped from the earth and planted back again, upside down. Torn branches and ravaged roots and disturbed earth had scattered everywhere. Reik felt sick at the carnage.

"It appears that he knows what we've been about," Tak'homa said wryly.

Anger surged. "Why should he care?" Reik raged. "It's not that I don't appreciate everything you've shown me," he told her. "It will all make me a better, more adaptable fighter—but none of it will really help against a mage of his caliber."

"It will help, if you *think* and use strategy against him. Use his instability to keep him engaged or frustrated. Take advantage of his reckless nature and quick temper." She heaved a sigh. "But what we've been doing is not what he thinks it is."

"What does he think?" he frowned.

"Runar sees that I have taken you under my wing. He knows that I am instructing you." She looked directly at him. "He thinks that I am giving you what he's been after, all of this time."

"What? What does he want?" Reik still felt mystified, and that feeling of being at a loss was only fueling his anger.

"Fire," she said simply.

He stared, dumbstruck. "Why in the world would he think that you could give him fire?"

"I am powerful." She shrugged. "Earth, air, and water, green life and animal life and wind and ice and light. They all make up my mountain. And deep in the roots of it lives a core of molten destruction, a kind of power that both destroys and gives life. I am of it. It is of me. I hold sway over it all."

Reik blinked.

"Runar is powerful, too. He may be the greatest ice mage that has ever walked the earth. Yet it is not enough for him. He wants to rule fire as well as ice. He thinks I can share the secret of how to manage both—and he thinks that it will make him invincible."

"It might! You must not give it to him."

"I won't. He is too volatile, too impatient, too quick to turn to violence and destruction already." She gestured to the devastation around them. "Holding the secret to fire would not improve him. Not at all."

Reik started to respond. But something—a whisper on the wind?—made him stop and jump back, some instinct prompting him to boost his movement with a blast of ice.

With a crash, an uprooted tree landed where he'd just been standing.

A roar sounded nearby. Reik shouted over it. "Tak'homa!"

The spot where she had been was covered in swaying branches.

She walked out of the trembling mass, unscathed. "He cannot harm me with what is mine."

Her eyes flashed. Her color mounted. Reik registered the anger growing in her, but Runar hadn't finished. He strode out of the woods, his arms raised, and sent a group of glittering spikes racing toward him. Almost without thought, Reik threw up a thick wall. The spikes struck, shattering against it, just inches from him.

"He aims at you?" Tak'homa spat in fury. "His own flesh?" Her voice echoed across the open space.

Runar shifted back into White Shoulders. He roared back at her, his fangs bared.

The mountain spirit took a wide stance. She seemed to grow larger as she tossed her head back and sang something into the sky.

She threw her arms apart. A pit opened up directly beneath the Yeti. He let out a yelp as he fell in. Tak'homa clapped her hands together and the earth closed over his head.

Reik gasped. He took a step forward, then turned back to her. "You will bury him alive?"

"No," she said smugly. "I'm taking a leaf from his own book. That track of ice that carried you to the pond was an unusual and effective idea. I just tweaked it a little."

"Tweaked?" he rasped. "How?"

"I just made a tunnel of earth to carry him back and spit him out at the cave he's camped in. Maybe he'll pack up and go."

Reik slumped. "He won't."

"I know." She sighed. "But as the humans say . . . A girl can dream, no?"

He wished he could summon a smile.

"Let's go, then." She turned away. "We have plans to make."

# CHAPTER 9

Tak'homa took him back out to the slope above her son's resting place. She produced a steaming hot mug of tea. He took it and sat out on the outcropping.

She cleared her throat. "Families can be difficult."

She waited a moment and when he didn't respond, she gave a shrug. "My parents are the wide sky and the great earth mother, so I cannot claim that our problems are the same. But I've had issues aplenty with my husband." She waited again. "Shockingly, I don't think your parents are the worst I've seen."

He huddled over the mug and stared out at the range of mountains beyond the peak.

"It's time," she said gently. "We must talk openly, despite your disinclination."

Reik only watched the cloud shadows moving across the stark landscape.

Tak'homa did not relent. "You are young. Incredibly talented, but so very young."

The silence stretched out a moment longer.

"Humans," she said, pursing her lips. "There are so very

many of you, and in seemingly infinite variations. The one thing that binds you, though, and makes you all so admirable, is your great capacity for love." Her gaze narrowed. "It is the ones among you who do not, or cannot, embrace that, who become the most dangerous."

"My father doesn't love me," Reik said at last.

"That much is apparent."

"He doesn't even know me. He never tried to."

"He is a lost cause," Tak'homa acknowledged. "He chose his path long ago. But he is not your only parent."

He looked away again.

"In spite of your youth, you have enough experience to know that there are vast differences among spiritual creatures, just as with humans. *Kami* and *yokai* and elementals and spirits and others in between." She looked directly at him. "Not all of them have the capacity for love, or for any type of emotional connection. That makes us dangerous, as well."

"My mother does love me," he bit out.

"I know . . . that she does care for you in her own way. The best way that she is able to. I cannot see the messages she sends you in your sleep, but I can feel the urgency and the concern that comes with them. Just as I can feel the turmoil they leave behind in you." Her shoulders hunched a bit. "What I don't know . . . and now must ask . . . is why? Why you are here, if it is at her bidding? She is Inaba's creature. Has she sent you here to try and recruit me to his side?"

Reik choked on a mouthful of tea.

"Or have you been sent to evaluate my weaknesses? To test the limits of my powers?"

He made a sound of protest. "I am not aligned with Inaba!"

She raised a brow at him. "I know about Yuki Onna, Reik. I know that she is no longer purely a *yokai*. She has become

66

something *between* mortal and spirit." Her tone grew sharper. "And I know how she was made that way."

He stilled.

"I see that you know, as well."

He nodded.

"We have been aware of Inaba for longer than most, those of us who are linked to the Earth. You have heard the story in your village of Ryu, I am sure. But we felt it, long ago, those moments of his transformation into something more than a man, because he accomplished it through the power of an earth mage, by stealing the power and magic from the Earth itself. We suffered a day or so of real terror and determination, because we knew we could not allow him to succeed."

She sighed. "But Rialka intervened and trapped him in the spirit world and we all breathed in relief. For many years I did not think of him again. Yes, we heard rumors of his rising, of his growing dominion over much of the spirit world, of so many *yokai* and spirits falling under his influence. Stories of your mother circulated, too. Tales of the ruthless Yuki Onna who acted as his right hand. But it all seemed so far away. I am here. Of this place. I spared little thought for him." Her head drooped. "Until I heard my friend's shout. A call of horror and pain—followed by utter silence."

Reik winced. He knew whom she meant. The spirit of the volcanic mountain south of here.

"Yes. I can see that you know the story." Sorrow washed over her lined face.

"Mount Saint Helens," Reik whispered.

"So she was called by the modern men. But I will tell you the parts of the tale that you do not know." She set her shoulders. "Her name was Loowit. She was a lively, curious woman. We kept each other company for many years. She could be so kind and her laughter was impossible to resist.

She had a temper, though, that was quick to rise high, although it burned out just as fast."

She paused a moment, her gaze turning south and west. "I know now what happened. She was sleeping when Inaba sent a party of his creatures to her lair. Scientists. An earth mage. And your mother."

"It was before I was born . . ."

"It was before you were able to be born," she corrected. "We know now that my friend was one of the victims of Inaba's experiments, his attempts to find a way back into the mortal world. But your mother was a different sort of victim. Yuki Onna went into Loowit's home a pure *yokai*. But by the time they finished their work—their experiments—one of the first of the major natural disasters that woke the Ring of Fire had struck and Loowit was gone. And your mother was something else . . .something new. A *yokai* who had somehow also become mortal."

"Tethered to the mortal world," Reik corrected. "Part of her is trapped in an object here in the mortal world. Whoever possesses the object holds her in his grasp."

"And Runar has it?"

He shouldn't tell her. But he owed her. More than that— he trusted her. "Runar has it. But Inaba *thinks* that he has it. The object he has is a fake, but he doesn't know."

She let loose a long breath. "Your mother is serving two difficult masters, then."

"Yes."

"And that is why she sent you?"

"She didn't send me! She forbade me to even look for Runar! But I wouldn't have it. Inaba no longer trusts her. I asked her to spare a friend of mine—someone Inaba wanted badly. She did it, for my sake, and he has been treating her differently since then." He closed his eyes. "He's looking back,

68

too. I think he suspects that it was she who released me, when I was small."

"Released you?"

"Yes. I was born in Inaba's lair in JanFran. I spent my first years there, in the labs." He swallowed heavily before he could go on. "She got me out. She left me in the one place he couldn't find me."

"Ryu."

He nodded.

"Then she does care for you . . ."

"As I've said. And as you said, she cares . . . as much as she is able."

"Then what is upsetting you so? What is she sending you in your dreams?"

"I'm worried," he admitted. "It's like . . . she's trying to show me her life. Make me understand how it was for her, before Inaba ensnarled her. She showed me how she was trapped into his service."

The sun passed from behind a cloud and Tak'homa closed her eyes against the sudden ray of light. Or against her thoughts. "She's seeking your understanding, perhaps."

"That's what I'm afraid of!" he burst out. The anguish he'd been trying to ignore clawed its way out with the words. "Is she telling me her side of things? Does she know Inaba plans to be rid of her? Is she trying to . . . prepare me?"

Tak'homa considered it. "It could be," she answered reluctantly. "But there are other explanations. I've often wondered . . ." She eyed Reik directly. "You say she is showing you scenes from her long life. Her life before Inaba?"

"Yes."

"Do you think they are a true representation of her past?"

He thought about it. "Yes. I think she wants me to see the truth about her."

"Does she seem different to you? In those early days?"

"In what way?"

"Just think about what she's shown you. How is her manner different? Her affect? Even her movements or interests or temper?"

Reik shrugged. "I don't know. My mother is . . . not like you. She's always been a little distant." He thought about it. "But yes, if I had to say so, I think she might be even more remote in those early days. She doesn't listen to my warnings or pleas at all in the dreams. In real life she at least listens, even if she doesn't always see my way of things."

"What about her victims?" Tak'homa asked.

He nodded. "In the dreams—the past—she seems utterly unconcerned with her victims and the role she plays to lure them to their doom." He frowned and nodded. "Now, she does sometimes seem as if she is reluctant to feed—but she is resigned to it. Except she never seems to enjoy having to drain blood instead of chi." Out of honesty, he forced himself to add, "Although when her temper is riled, there have been times when she seemed to enjoy both."

Tak'homa's mouth twisted. "Well, considering how much I just relished dropping your father into a pit, we won't hold it against her." She grew serious. "I know there are other *yokai* that underwent the same process that your mother did, yes?"

He nodded. "A few more."

"I've listened for stories of them. Several were unstable after the change and didn't last long. One other seemed to be a success, although there were reports of personality changes."

"You mean the Tengu?"

"Yes. His effectiveness apparently wavered once he was part mortal. Your mother was by far the most successful of those experiments. I listened closely for stories of her, after Loowit disappeared. And they were plentiful. Everyone seemed eager to remark on the changes in her. Tales of her blood drinking were tossed about in horror, but others spoke of a thawing in her. It was even whispered that she now held some sympathy for those who defied her master."

Tak'homa turned her gaze south. "Her transformation was fueled by the earth's energy, stolen from Loowit and her mountain. I've often wondered if something of Loowit might have been transferred too. Perhaps that is why there was a softening of her nature. Perhaps part of my friend lives on in your mother.

Reik gazed south, too. "I don't know. You could be right."

"What you've told me of your mother strengthens my belief." With a nod, she turned back to him. "It makes me more determined to help you, as well."

"You have already helped me."

"Yes. Your friendship has been a boon to me as well, easing my loneliness and re-connecting me with the outside world." She drew a deep breath. "And now I wish to help you free Yuki Onna."

Reik blinked. "How?"

She pursed her lips. "You have come far to fight Runar. It would be wrong of me to step in and do it in your stead."

"No," he protested instinctively. "I mean, yes. It would be wrong."

"I will not take your chance at victory. Not when it would mean so much to both you and your mother. But I will help you." She clutched his shoulder. "I will try to give you what Runar seeks. I will train you to wield fire."

It turned out that *try* was the operative word. Reik was thrilled at the offer and more than willing to learn. Tak'homa talked to him at length about how fire *feels* different from ice.

How it breathed and danced with a life of its own. She guided him in extensive meditation, trying to help him find a place of energy inside him that would connect with the new element. She sat him next to the kitchen cook fire and a series of outdoor blazes, attempting to help him coax a flame to his palm.

Reik did try. The thought of bringing fire into a fight with his father spurred him to work and toil and try again and again. He wanted it to work. He needed to be successful.

But he could not make the connection. He didn't know how to explain it to Tak'homa, but ice was a part of him. And he, hard and brittle, alternately strong and fragile, had always felt at one with it. The whisper of it lived in his blood, flowed under his skin. It always stood ready and instantly responsive when he called.

He could find none of that affinity with fire.

But he kept trying.

Runar kept trying, too. Enraged at his defeat, he had not left the mountain. Instead, now that he knew about the misdirections, he kept searching, probing to find another, identifiable one.

"He'll make his way back in, eventually," Tak'homa said.

They talked between his efforts. Her willingness to help him finally opened a gate inside of him.

He told her of his foster parents, of his lessons at Ryu and the people of the village. He even told her a little about his friends.

Shockingly, it felt good. He didn't feel vulnerable or weak, as he feared. The sharing strengthened their bond of friendship and he gained clarity and insight into his own complicated feelings just by sorting and sharing them.

They spoke no more of his mother, however, and she no longer came to him in his dreams. And her absence, her silence, frightened him even more than the message she might have been trying to send him.

So he listened harder, trying to hear the fire's voice so he could learn to sing with it.

And then, one day, he felt something.

Tak'homa had taken him on another long walk. She showed him ridges of rock peeking through a couple of the glaciers on the mountain, and long sheets of it that showed beneath a few thin spots, as well.

"Lava flow," she told him. "Great layers of it make up large portions of my mountain." They walked on, through scrubby woods, until she halted on a small rocky slope bordering a clearing. The shelf of rock lay bare of growth, ice or snow. He could feel the warmth beneath his feet as they paused there.

"I have called a stream of magma close to the surface. It is not fire. But it is full of heat and power. Stay here. Experiment with it. See if there is a connection—but be sure to stay upwind and away from the gases that rise with it."

Intrigued, Reik nodded. He watched her shuffle off, smiling a little as she stopped to croon to a few hardy green things poking through the snow at the edge of the clearing. Then he turned to the small slope of exposed rock.

She was right. This was different. He could feel the flow of the lava beneath the surface almost in the same way that he could sense an underground source of water. The magma felt slower, to be sure. And incredibly hot—and almost alive in a way that he could not quite understand.

He shrugged. It was more success than he had met with before. He sank down and bent his head, straining, trying to hear the lava's voice.

Gradually, as the minutes passed, he did hear something. Faint and low and slow. Chanting? He closed his eyes. Slowly it became clearer. Lighter. Almost . . . feminine.

He lost focus suddenly as he realized the warmth under him had faded. His eyes popped open. Frowning, he looked down to see a patch of frost creeping across the bare rock. It reached his bent legs and began to creep up and over, in the same way the ice had done to his feet before Runar's cave.

Casting wildly about, he spotted his father stepping from the line of evergreens across the clearing. "Now, boy. There will be no spying, no skulking, and no hiding behind the old girl's skirts. Now, we talk."

The ice had sealed him to the rock. It continued to grow, heading past his calves for his shins.

*Stop*, he told it.

It climbed on, just as it had done before.

But now Reik closed his eyes once more. He reached for that center inside of him. Touched the energy that directed his talent, the whirling spot that connected him to the ice. Lifting a finger, he commanded the ice again.

This time the ice stopped climbing.

He could feel the conflicting magic. The element wavered, shook, torn in two directions.

*It's fine*, Reik soothed it. *We are together.*

Distress eased. The ice released him and began to retreat from the rock. Reik took his time climbing to his feet.

"Learned a few things from the old woman, did you?" Runar sneered. "You could have just come to me, boy. Approached me openly. No need to whore yourself out to the old girl."

"I'm not a fool." The first words he'd ever spoken to his father. "You would not have welcomed me."

Runar considered, lifting a shoulder. "You're probably right. I probably would have buried you in an avalanche when I got the first whiff of power off you. In fact . . ." He raised his hand.

Light in the clearing disappeared as a vast, roiling mass of snow and ice filled the sky, blocking the sun as it fell.

He didn't think, not really. He just threw his arm high, *seeing* the glittering, protective cone before it formed around him. The high end was pointed. Hard as a diamond. A spike of ice as cold as a polar cap, as hollow as the hole in his heart where his father's care should have been. It punched through the deluge like a fist while the widening sides of the cone encircled him, shunting the snow and ice away and keeping him safe.

When it ended, Reik threw his hands out. The structure shattered, hanging in the air like a million diamonds before it winked out, taking all of the avalanche material with it.

Runar frowned and his hand went up again.

Instinctive memory kicked in and Reik pinned it to the tree behind him with a multitude of tiny ice darts buried deep into the wood.

His father smirked and jerked his hand.

Nothing happened.

Runar snapped his head around to glare at his trapped arm. He narrowed his gaze and all of the spikes melted. They reformed instantly, flowing into a single, thin blade that surged toward Reik.

He ducked, then whipped his head up as he felt a surge of power.

Runar had moved away from the tree line. He stood, feet planted wide, arms spread. He pulled ice ribbons out of the air one after the other. Magic pulsed and fused with them as they swirled about him, encasing him in layers of protection and might.

Reik took a step back. He could feel the strength of it, growing and pressing on his skin. Runar's form was entirely covered, the ice molding itself into crude armor. Only his red eyes glowed from within.

It was too much. He couldn't fight this. Runar wasn't even finished with the spell and Reik knew he had nothing in his arsenal that would stand against it. He turned, thinking that he could run, head for the cave while his father finished turning himself into a weapon.

"Oh, no, you don't."

Before he'd even reached the far end of the open space, Runar jumped to stop him. His great arm flew and hit Reik with a backhanded blow. He flew back to the center of the clearing and landed face first in a spray of snow.

His father followed, his arm swinging again even as an icy cudgel formed in his hand.

Reik rolled as it came crashing down. It missed him by a hair and sent another shower of snow into the air. He kept rolling and came up into a crouch, wielding his own club. The two met in mid-swing and broke apart, falling away.

Runar swung his fist and Reik scrambled back and out of the way. He'd reached the bare rock where he'd begun. It still felt a little warm under his hands as he rolled to push to his feet.

"Enough games." Runar's voice sounded strangely amplified from within his armor. He set his foot on Reik's shoulders and pushed him down again.

He struggled, but the imprint of his father's foot grew, spreading across his back. The growing weight of it pressed him flat.

"Inaba will have a far easier time with you in the spirit world," his father growled.

Air squeezed out of him. Reik struggled, blindly sending blasts backwards over his shoulder, but Runar only laughed at his feeble attempts.

The rock was warm against his cheek. Strange that his end would come with warmth—and stranger still that he would find comfort in it. His breathing became shallow. He winced as his ribs creaked in protest. The magma flowed just inches below and he let his mind travel with it. The chanting. There it was. He let it swell up inside of him.

He'd thought that the stream felt alive before. Now he sensed that it was more. Heat and earth and life and death, they all roiled together in that glowing stream. There was something else there, too. *Someone* else.

*Yes, Reik. Here I am.*

It was her. Tak'homa. She was beneath him and she was in his head and she was . . . vast. So much more than he had expected. Her past stretched out behind her, a stream of love and sorrow, full of days and nights, music and laughter, tears and kindness and anger. So many people, animals and spirits gone in and out of her life. And power, incredible depths of it, drawn from wind and sky and rain and life and rooted deep, deep in the earth.

*Reach for me.*

He couldn't. Pain stabbed him and his body jerked in a spasmodic rhythm. His ribs were cracking, one by one.

*You can. Open your eyes.*

He did. She was everywhere. The light of her shone in all the life on the mountain.

*We are friends. True friends. We can make our own connection, Reik. But you must make the choice.*

A tiny light shone at the edge of the volcanic rock. An intrepid weed, fighting for life. Like all the rest, it pulsed with her essence.

*Yes. Touch it. Make the connection. Do it, Reik, and I will grant you use of my fire.*

The lava. The power that flowed straight from the earth's core . . .

*Yes.*

But he could see so much of her. There wasn't nearly as much to him. And most of it was petty and small. She would see it all, his fears and his mistakes and inadequacies. She would see him right through to his soul.

*Yes. But I know you already, as you have learned to know me.*

He hesitated. And then cringed at his own weakness. Would he die rather than expose himself? Would he not even try? That was not who he wanted to be. He crept his fingers toward the plant. It hurt. Everything hurt. Things were popping and squishing inside of him. His lungs were filling up.

Suddenly, the mountain shook.

Runar struggled to keep his balance. His foot lifted. The pressure eased.

And Reik grabbed that tiny, insignificant plant.

He screamed.

Too much. The force of it ripped through him. Too much, too fast. All of his wounds healed in one excruciating second. He was pulled in a thousand directions. Every cell in his body expanded, charged with energy and potential—for life and for destruction.

Rolling over, he grabbed his father's foot as it tried to descend on him again—and he chose destruction.

He channeled the heat and the power, sent it surging against the combined might of ice and magic.

Runar's red eyes widened. Ribbons began to unfurl and evaporate away. Magic ebbed, putting up a fight, but it was a small wave battling against an immense wall. It flowed away in defeat and Runar's armor began to dissolve into steam beneath Reik's hands.

His father tugged and thrashed, but Reik held on. All of the armor was wisping away now. Runar began to struggle in earnest, kicking and fighting. The last of the ice evaporated. Reik gripped bare skin now.

Runar screamed.

He should let go. Reik knew he should. But all the anger and hurt he felt for his father tightened his fingers instead.

He closed his eyes against the sudden flare of light—and suddenly it was a Yeti's muscular leg he held on to. The creature roared and began to beat him about the head and shoulders. Reik threw up a thick shield. He was ice above and fire below. He squeezed and turned his head away from the sickening scent of burning hair and flesh.

*Enough, now.*

He had to let go. He knew it.

Anger surged in denial. Dredged up his mother's misery. His own misery, during all the nights he'd lain awake, wondering why his father didn't want to know anything about him. He could use it. Squeeze and squeeze until his father burned like a torch against the evening sky.

No. Not him. Not him.

This wasn't him.

He let go.

Runar stumbled back, his eyes wide and his fangs gleaming in menace. He glared at Reik for a moment, then he turned and loped off into the trees.

Groaning, Reik got to his feet, Tak'homa appearing suddenly at his side to assist. "Well, that didn't go quite as planned."

He held on to her, gripping her hand when she might have let him go.

"Thank you."

She gave him a nod and a smile. "You fought well. But you won by defeating one of your greatest fears. We are connected now." She patted his arm. "Your mother would be proud."

Tears threatened, but it was his mother he must think of now. "He's heading for the cave. I'll never beat him there."

Tak'homa frowned—but then her brow rose and she

grinned. "You will arrive first—if you allow me to send you back as I did him, last time."

Through the earth. Reik shuddered at the idea, his skin crawling at the idea of being buried alive. But he nodded. "Quickly. Please."

Her hand slid down to hold his tight. "My fire—it is heat and stone and its own sort of magic. I give you leave to use it in this fight."

He blinked back tears again. "Thank you. For everything."

"It will only work for you here, on my mountain. So finish this at last."

He nodded. "I will. It is time."

She let go and stepped back. "Hold your breath," she advised. "It won't last long."

Then she clapped her hands.

# CHAPTER 10

R eik did hold his breath—and he kept his mouth and eyes shut tight too—and he still cringed through the entire underground trip, which thankfully did not last long.

He felt even more thankful when the journey ended—gratified when he popped out of a wall and found himself already inside Runar's cave. Stumbling, he crouched, blinking and finding his bearings on his feet and in the dim light.

The place was dark and nearly empty—not at all like Tak'homa's homey cavern.

A pile of pelts, indifferently cured and more than a little rank, lay just behind him. Beyond that, in the farthest reaches of the cave, he glimpsed a pile of bones. Small mammals mostly, but propped near the front sat a flat disc of bone. The flash of recognition jarred him. It looked like the odd, disconnected faceplate of the Ijirac's first form.

Shaking his head, he looked further. A fire pit ringed in stone had been placed near the entrance. Next to it sat the large cook pot he'd seen and a couple of smaller ones. No plates or silverware that he could see.

There was nothing else. No boxes or drawers or back-packs where his mother's snow globe might be hidden.

It made no sense. His mother knew that Runar carried the object with him on his travels. She'd tried to steal it several times before. Yet it wasn't the sort of object to keep on your person. It must be hidden here somewhere.

But there was nothing else. Only a flat, dirt floor and rough, irregular rocky walls.

Reik paused. Perhaps that it was it. He looked at the dirt carefully, searching for signs of digging, but found none. He pursed his lips. There were several outcroppings of rock protruding into the room, however. Moving to the middle of the space, he blew out an icy breath. *Only on the true rock,* he instructed the frost that began to form.

He blew until sparkling white frost coated the ceiling and all of the walls, except for one larger boulder opposite the pelts. It remained rough and dark and frost-free.

He crossed to kneel before it, his mind whirling as he considered how he might break the protective spell. Freeze and shatter? A sharp drill to—

No need. It was merely an illusion. As he touched the surface, it melted away.

Beneath sat an old trunk, square, with brass fittings and a large lock. Reik rolled his eyes. Blasting locks was one of the first things they'd taught him in Inaba's labs. It shattered in an instant. Heart pounding, he lifted the lid.

From the top he pulled a couple of furs, rich and fine, unlike the ones piled behind him. Beneath lay Runar's collected treasures.

Not so many, for such a long life. But Reik imagined that what his father truly valued was the magic and power he could manipulate. Maybe these held some sentimental value?

He pulled out a dagger, magnificently curved, with a bone handle and a Damascus steel blade etched with a rose near the hilt. Next came a wide, golden armband carved with raven symbols and then a strand of colorful beads intersected with spiral shells. The bottom of the chest was covered in ancient silver coins, rough-hewn and dingy. He shoved his hand in, searching—and pulled out the snow globe.

*Yes.*

Reik clutched it to his chest, something inside of him bursting in triumph and relief.

But he couldn't celebrate yet. He had to get it out, get it away from Runar in order to truly set his mother free. He paused long enough to wrap the globe in one of the furs and tuck it in his shirt. He dashed for the opening of the cave—

Only to stop himself at the edge, before he stepped out into the pristine clearing. He peered about, looking for signs of Runar.

Nothing.

Still, he remembered last time. Booby traps.

With a wave of his hand, he dropped a barrage of icicles onto the clean snow.

He startled, jumping back as an ice-crafted bear trap leapt up and out of the snow, snapping shut right in front of him. Two more did the same beyond it, and several tripped snares triggered the launch of various sharp objects from trees.

The slow burn of anger in his gut suddenly surged, lifted higher by his feelings of urgency and impatience. He was so close. Runar would not stop him now.

Closing his eyes, he braced himself on the edge of the cave opening. The rock pulsed with Tak'homa's energy, but a bit fainter than it had through the living plant. Fine. He called it and it came in a slower wave, more manageable.

Reik clenched his fist until it glowed red, then opened it to cup a living flame. Concentrating fiercely, he sent a large tongue of heat and fire out, sweeping it across the clearing, melting away the ice and snow and any magic linked to it.

When it was done, he stepped out into a steaming field of earth and stone. Another step. One more. Before he'd reached the middle, he was running, sprinting to get to Tak'homa's territory. The globe would be safe from Runar behind her shields.

The dry heat in the air made it easier to feel the blast of cold heading for his back.

Whirling, he met the arctic missile with his own blast of fire. The impact let loose a spectacular display of sparks, mist and steam.

"Brat!" The call came from above. Reik scanned the skies, both hands raised and ready. When he finally spotted his father, he forgot to fire a return volley.

His mouth dropped. Runar was in his human form. His injured leg had been encased in a bandage of ice that resembled a cast. But that wasn't what gripped Reik and left him staring in awe and begrudging admiration.

*Wings.* From his father's back sprouted a massive, grand pair of wings. They shone like crystal, the carved detail of each functional feather apparent even from a distance. And Runar used them like he'd been born with them, climbing and wheeling like a great bird of prey.

What discipline must have crafted those? What magic must have helped? What a huge amount of work and practice it must have taken to look so effortless.

For moment, Reik was paralyzed by a gut-wrenching sense of loss. What might he have learned from Runar, had he been a different kind of man? What adventures might they have had together, father and son?

Runar showed himself *not* to be harboring any such sentimentality by swinging by and firing off another icy blast at Reik's side.

He countered it with a swipe of his fiery hand.

For a moment, it was like a dance. On partner taunting, turning on a wing, climbing high and swooping low, firing blast after blast of winter. Runar sent cyclones after him, and threw ice boulders, tossed freezing winds and tiny knives. Reik just kept turning on the ground. Silent. Focused. Moving and wielding flame to null the attacks.

At last, Runar settled on the ridge above the cave. "It's only that fire that gives you a fighting chance, damn you. And damn Tak'homa too, for giving it to you, after I spent years asking, chanting and sacrificing to her." He sneered. "What did you have to give her, boy, to get that fire?"

Reik stood straight, both fists clenched. "My friendship."

His father rolled his eyes. "Well, then, damn me too, for I had to give your mother a damned sight more than that to gain Inaba's favor and make sure you were spawned." His wings began to beat again, although he didn't take to the sky. "I helped bring you into the world, thinking you would be Inaba's creature and no trouble to me. Yet here you are, a thorn in my side—so I am happy to take you out, too." He began to beat faster, blowing up a wind. His hands moved in a circle. A glowing ball of blue light formed between them. "In fact, I think both of you have become more trouble than you are worth. I'm going to take back that snow globe, boy, and I'm going to deliver it to Inaba. I'm going to tell him he's had a fake all of this time—and while I'm at it, I'll inform him that Yuki Onna was the one to steal you away from his labs, all those years ago."

"No!" Reik brought both fists up, one still glowing red. "He'll destroy her!"

"And I'll laugh while he does it." The wind blew harder now. Lightning and snow and lashing gales lived in the ball that grew between his hands. Abruptly, Runar tossed it at him. It expanded as it came, rushing on that wind. Reik raised his hands in defense, and Runar watched the fiery one, wary of what might come out of it.

So Reik used the other to launch a long lance of ice straight for his father's shoulder. It struck, piercing muscle and shattering bone and traveled on to impale the shining wing at his back.

Runar screamed.

The wing fell, drooping with the sound of a falling chandelier.

The icy ball of storm and lightning, as tall as Reik now, collapsed just before it hit him.

His father was listing, stumbling as he tried to pull the lance out. Groaning, he put a hand on it and after several moments, it melted away. Runar sagged, his uninjured wing fluttering while the other dragged him down. His bad leg gave way and he fell heavily to the bare earth below the ridge.

Reik took a step toward him. The wings disappeared.

Runar didn't move. Another step—and his father rolled over, wielding a line of ice like a whip, hitting Reik in the knees and knocking him over.

He tried to rise, but Runar had a hand in the air and the injured arm braced on the ground. Winter rushed toward him from both, wrapping him a blanket of cold, freezing him to the earth.

Reik countered with Tak'homa's fire, melting Runar's freezing layers even as his father struggled to add more. They were locked in a stalemate, their powers cancelling each other out. Neither could win. Neither *would* win until someone dropped from sheer exhaustion.

A fine mist began to build up behind Runar. Snow drifted down upon them both. Reik braced himself. A last trick up his father's sleeve?

It was not. He gasped as Yuki Onna materialized behind

Runar. She crouched behind him on the ground. Her eyes locked with Reik's, then she leaned down and bit into his father's neck.

Runar yelled in surprise and pain. His attack fell off. Jerking himself away, he struggled to get to his feet. "You! Damn it! I should have known! This is all your fault." He sneered. "A fine thing for a mother to hide behind her son's feeble powers." He shook out a walking stick of ice and used it to steady himself.

Yuki Onna raised her hand. "No. I did not send our son here. He came himself. Can you not see? He did it out of regard for me—and curiosity about you."

Runar laughed. "Then his curiosity will get you both killed." He tossed the stick at her. It turned razor thin as it hurled toward her face.

She dodged it easily, moving above the earth in that smooth way of hers. Limping, Runar pursued her, tossing one attack after another with one hand, his injured arm pressed tight to his chest. She avoided some, and turned others back, her long, ebony locks flowing and acting independently, as Reik had seen them do before. They snatched spikes and knives from the air and sent them back at Runar.

"Leave her alone!" Reik followed them, watching for an opening. She shouldn't have come. His mother had no real defenses against Runar. Yes, snow often followed her but she could not summon or control it. She had no attack to fend him off and no sort of defense except her quick maneuverability.

She'd floated high to thwart Runar's throws. He began to fling ice axes at her, sending them whirling end over end with the ease of experience. Reik flinched as one twirled past her and nicked her in the arm. She clutched it, looking shocked at the flow of red down her arm. She began to sink lower and Reik blinked. She'd had one foot in the mortal world for nineteen years. Was this the first time she'd seen her own blood?

Runar took advantage of her hesitation and stalked toward her with a sword in hand, raised high.

"No!" Reik shouted, coming up behind him. "Stop!"

He shot a blast of intense heat at Runar, thinking to melt the sword.

Runar jumped back, his weapon vanished and his good hand gone red. With a snarl, his father turned on him. He shot a mound of snow at Reik's feet to trip him up and a spike of ice to intercept him as he fell.

Reik couldn't stop his fall. He couldn't deflect the spike—his arms had flung instinctively wide when he'd tripped. He could see it coming. It was going to end him.

It didn't matter. Yuki Onna wouldn't leave him while he lived. With him dead, she could take the globe and disappear —free at last.

He closed his eyes, waiting to feel cold death hit him.

And opened them again at the sound of a thud and a grunt.

"No!" he sobbed. "Mother!" He reached for her. She had dropped quickly from her spot on high and right into the path of the spike. Slick with blood, it protruded through her upper abdomen. "Mother," he whispered.

She fell against him and he lowered her gently to the ground, touched her face, took her hand. "No. I wanted you to be free at last . . ."

"She's *yokai*, you dolt." Runar advanced on them. "Immortal. She'll be sent back to the spirit world."

Fury and grief exploded out of Reik. Coalesced into a burning hot wind, they hit Runar and knocked him backward and off of his feet.

"She is not *yokai*," Reik spat. "She is *unique*. A blend of mortal and spirit that has never been seen before and no one truly understands! There is no way to know what will happen to her if she dies here in the mortal world."

"I don't care!" Runar raged. "I don't care if she dies or if she is flung to the farthest reaches of the spirit world, never to return!" His expression turned crafty as he rose to his feet. "But I will have that globe back, you ungrateful brat, so that if she does return, it will be to her place—under my thumb." He moved toward them, calling up a polar wind that was the opposite match to Reik's last blow. "Hand over the globe and anything else you've taken from me." His mouth twisted into a snarl. "Or don't. And I will take it when your mother bleeds out and you are scattered into a million pieces."

Something snapped as that cold wind surged past Reik. The last, forlorn hope that this could end with both of them intact. He looked down at his broken mother, saw her shallow breaths coming too quickly, and he stood.

Flame, fierce and hot and as never ending as his sorrow, rushed out of him. It flared high and wide, surrounding his father completely, encircling him.

Runar cringed, caught, unable to move as Reik surrounded him with the molten flow. But Reik would not relent. He added layer after layer, chilling and cooling each one until Runar was entombed in volcanic rock, and then, to add insult, he finished with a thick layer of ice.

It was over in a few seconds. His father was trapped and his mother . . .

He dropped to his knees.

Somehow, she smiled at him. "You are a fine son," she whispered. One hand reached for him. "You see, I do care for you."

"As I love you, Mother. I always have."

Her gaze wandered. "I will go to the spirit world. I feel it calling me." She stopped, panting a moment and her gaze returned to him. "I will be weakened. It will be long . . .

before I can cross into the mortal world . . . before we see each other again."

"I don't care. I will carry you with me. I will always love you."

She sighed. "I know I have not been the mother . . . that you . . . wished. I have tried. But you should know . . . you have been . . . my greatest gift."

Tears welled. One slipped off his cheek and the icy pellet dropped into her open hand.

She smiled and her eyes closed. "You must tell her," she whispered. "Your friend. The Girl with the Stars . . . Tell her all that has happened here. Everything. Share what I showed you. Inaba . . . his early life. She must see, she must know, before she faces him."

Her body arched. The lovely sheen of her skin began to fade. "Tell your friend . . . here . . ." She fought for breath. "Loowit remembers her. And I will . . ."

He waited. "Mother?"

"I will . . . remember you."

Her last breath eased out of her. Reik choked on a sob and clutched her close, knowing what might happen, and flinching to see that it had already begun. But it was different than he'd seen with other *yokai*. All the outlines of her body glowed bright for an instant, and then darkened to utter black. The blackness spread, moving inward and in its wake her form turned to grey, sparkling dust. The black whirled down into a tight spiral, pulling all the dust with it—and with a *pop*—it all disappeared.

## EPILOGUE

How long he sat there, staring at the spot where his mother had been, he didn't know. But a brilliant sunset lit the sky behind Tak'homa when she appeared next to him and touched his shoulder.

"I am so very sorry," she said quietly.

Heaving a great sigh, he looked up at her. "Your friend Loowit remembers you."

Her face softened and she moved to sit beside him. Together they watched the sun sink behind the ridge. And when night bloomed, she led him away. Much as she'd done on that first day, Tak'homa took him to her home and let him rest.

He slept and slept. And when he couldn't sleep any longer, he sat up and faced the first day without his mother in it. After he'd bathed and eaten, they went back to the clearing before the cave and stood before the iced-over sphere.

"He's still alive in there, you know."

"I know."

"And spitting mad."

"Good."

"What are you going to do with him?"

"Nothing, for now. Let him rot in there for a bit." He turned to her. "I have to go."

Sighing, she nodded.

"I promised to meet a friend. And then . . . I have to do as my mother asked."

"And what did she ask?"

"She left another message for me to deliver."

"I see."

"I hate to ask it," he gestured at the sphere. "Can I leave him here? Will you watch over him until I am ready to deal with him?"

She made a face. "I'm not so thrilled to keep him close, but for you, I will." Sighing, she gestured toward the cave. "I can seal him in there, if you like. Prevent him from leaving— or communicating."

Reik glanced at the sphere. "Yes, move him, then," he bit out. He spun on his heel. "In a day or two."

The next afternoon, he bid Tak'homa goodbye—and just managed not to cry, in doing it.

"I will return," he promised.

Her mouth twisted. "I know. For him."

"Actually, I'd hoped you wouldn't mind if I came . . . for me. Perhaps, often?" He pressed the object in her hand. "And I would like for you to have this."

The fur fell away from the globe and she stared in surprise. "Reik? Are you sure? I know what this means to you."

"Your friendship means much to me, as well." Smiling, he nodded. "I'd like for you to remember me. And I'd like to think of it here, with you."

She returned his smile with a soft one of her own. "In that

case, very well. I am honored. We will both be waiting for you to return."

He left then, shouldering his pack and getting used to the heft of it again as he trekked down the mountain. His thoughts weighed heavier, though. Where would he find his friends? Mei, Ken, Hitomi and Sho had left Ryu. They followed the most dangerous path—straight to JanFran—and from his mother's urgency, he figured he should try to intercept them before they got there. He couldn't be sure of his reception—warm and fuzzy had never been his nature—but he would push and Mei, at least, should be open to hearing him. He only hoped that the information would mean something to her, that she would know what to do with it—and that it would somehow give meaning to his mother's loss.

He knew the moment he left the mountain. He faltered a little as the low, warm hum of Tak'homa's power drained away, but he straightened his shoulders and kept going. He was going to do as his mother asked. He was going to go out and choose a side.

*Reik, you chose long ago. If you hadn't, you would have left your mother to her fate.*

He supposed that Tak'homa was right, and for some reason, the thought cheered him. With a little smile and a nod that he hoped his mother might feel, he continued on.

# A NOTE FROM THE AUTHOR

Thank you for reading *The Fire in the Ice.* I hope you enjoyed it!

If you would like to hear when the next book in the series is out, enjoy sneak peeks and occasional freebies, and learn about the creatures and world of the Eye of the Ninja Chronicles, then sign up for my newsletter at www.dmmarlowe.com!

## ABOUT THE AUTHOR

D.M. Marlowe lives in North Carolina with her family and two cats. When she is not spoiling them all, she is probably writing. A proud geek, history buff and story addict, you can otherwise find her lost in a book or a movie, on a long walk, gardening or hanging with her friends.

In her other author life, she is a USA Today Bestselling author of Historical Romance for adults.

www.dmmarlowe.com
dmmarlowe@dmmarlowe.com

ALSO BY D.M. MARLOWE

Don't Miss the other books in the Eye of the Ninja Chronicles:

Eye of the Ninja

Obsidian's Eye

And coming soon:

In Her Mind's Eye